SPEAK NO EVIL

By Mignon Warner

SPEAK NO EVIL

MIGNON WARNER

PUBLISHED FOR THE CRIME CLUB
BY
DOUBLEDAY & COMPANY, INC.
GARDEN CITY, NEW YORK
1985

All of the characters in this book
are fictitious, and any resemblance
to actual persons, living or dead,
is purely coincidental.

Library of Congress Cataloging in Publication Data

Warner, Mignon.
Speak no evil.

I. Title.
RP6073.A7275S6   1984   823'.914
ISBN 0-385-19629-6
Library of Congress Catalog Card Number 84-10226

First Edition

SPEAK NO EVIL

CHAPTER ONE

At one-fifteen in the afternoon the man, a stranger to the village, was in the churchyard gazing intently at the church roof. As there was no longer any lead up there, the vicar did not consider there was any immediate cause for concern but was nevertheless relieved to find, when checking on the stranger's whereabouts a few minutes later, that he had disappeared.

At five past two Stan North, an amateur entomologist and the local unofficial weatherman, saw the same man slinking along the side of the bungalow belonging to the celebrated clairvoyante Edwina Charles. Stan North, who was occupied at the time with the insect life in the wood at the bottom of Mrs. Charles's garden, glanced up now and again, keeping an eye out for the man, but lost interest in him when the pair of ladybirds he had been observing began to mate. All the same, he felt it incumbent upon him to make some mention of the stranger to Margaret Sayer, one of the clairvoyante's near neighbours, when he met her outside her cottage gate an hour or so later. This was not perhaps the wisest of choices. Miss Sayer's antagonism towards the thrice-wed clairvoyante in particular, and fortune-telling in general, was legendary. Predictably, therefore, the elderly spinster merely listened to what Stan North had to say, made a small, disparaging snorting noise through her nose at the mention of Edwina Charles's name and the fact that Stan North knew for certain that the clairvoyante was not in when "the prowler" (as Stan North was now referring to him) called on her, and then continued through the gate to her front door. Stan North, his conscience somewhat eased for having shared the burden of this vaguely worrisome knowledge, watched her for a moment, then drifted over to the hedgerows and contentedly occupied himself there.

Once inside, Miss Sayer made straight for the drawer in the sideboard in her sitting room where the family silver was kept. It was all there. So was the tissue paper–wrapped pair of diminutive Victorian crystal bud vases that she liked to think was valuable. She hesitated, though, as she moved to close the drawer. Her opera glasses—the ones which had belonged to her grandmother and which Miss Sayer admitted to using principally in her bursts of sporadic surveillance of the activities in and about Mrs. Charles's home further down the road . . . Where were they?

She plunged her small hands back into the drawer, pushed some things aside, poked, and probed, all the while muttering angrily to herself about the sheer utter uselessness of men. (Stan North and Colonel Billingsley in particular—the latter having graphically described to the ladies and gentlemen of the Day Centre the suspicious behaviour of the shifty-looking cove he had encountered round the back of the library as he was taking a shortcut through the library gardens.)

Finally, quivering with rage—and with such ferocity that the sideboard rocked back and forth on its short, stubby Queen Anne legs—Miss Sayer closed the drawer. Then she marched over to the telephone, snatched up the receiver, and dialled her nephew David's number.

"I've been robbed," she announced without preamble. "By one of that-woman-up-the-road's old flames. I've no doubt he's been into every house in the village. Made himself a nice little haul, I shouldn't wonder!"

The man as good as admitted as much to the clairvoyante. Not necessarily that he had stolen anything on his leisurely passage through the village that afternoon, but that he had occupied his time while awaiting her return by visiting most of the houses along the road.

"It's true," he said as he followed the slim, attractive blond woman through to her office. "You country folk don't lock your doors when you go out."

Mrs. Charles gestured toward a chair and he sat down. Her voice when she spoke was abrupt.

"Edwin sent you, I believe you said."

The man looked at her meditatively. And that makes two of us, he thought. She didn't like Eddie Charles either. It was easy to see what he had seen in her: she had class, all right—and looks—but it was a mystery what she had seen in an old lag like Eddie. And yet there must have been something there once. Why else would she have kept his surname and use the feminine of his Christian name instead of her own given name of Adele?

Mrs. Charles continued in a dry voice, "That can only mean he owes you money." She unlocked a drawer in her desk and took out a cheque-book and pen. "How much is it this time?"

The man considered her for a moment. "Five hundred pounds," he replied.

Her blue eyes hardened. "Two-fifty," she countered, removing the top of her pen.

He watched her write out the cheque. "I'll leave you to fill in a name," she said, handing it to him. "See you don't come back."

He examined the cheque carefully before slowly tearing it into small pieces, which he then deposited in a neat pile on a corner of the desk.

He leaned back in his chair, folded his arms, then shook his head and softly clacked his tongue. "Our Mr. C. has really got his hooks into you, hasn't he? I thought he might have. . . . All them big important names he used to accidentally-on-purpose let drop—M.P.s, toffs . . . Clients of yours, he said. Made it sound as if you and them was bosom pals."

Mrs. Charles looked at him steadily. "I get the distinct impression that you're here to blackmail me, Mr.—whatever your name is. I would be obliged if you would get straight down to business. What is it you want of me if it isn't money to repay some debt of my ex-husband's?"

He smiled faintly as he replied.

"I've got a little job for you."

She gave him a searching look.

"You are a private eye, aren't you? Mr. C. said you were. Murder, he said . . . that's your speciality. Catching killers."

"I wouldn't necessarily believe everything Edwin told you, Mr. . . . ?"

"Valentine," he replied, his gaze straying momentarily to the squat metal safe standing squarely in the left-hand corner of the room. A smile flickered briefly in his light brown eyes when he looked back at the clairvoyante and saw that she had noted his interest. "A mere passing interest. Nothing more, I assure you," he said with a dismissive wave of his hand. "Some people admire paintings. Me . . ." He grinned. "I like safes."

He folded his arms again and looked at the clairvoyante steadily. When she remained silent, he said, "I want you to catch me a killer."

"You have someone specific in mind, or will any old killer do?" she inquired.

He nodded slowly, then grinned. "Yes . . . You and me are going to get along just fine." He paused, and the grin faded. "A couple of months back, a mate of mine—a real good pal, one of the best—was done in. I want you to find the swine that done it."

"You'll forgive me for being personal, Mr. Valentine—"

"Jimmy," he corrected her. "Just call me Jimmy."

The clairvoyante hesitated momentarily; then, continuing, "As you are obviously a close associate of my ex-husband, I should've thought you would be far better placed than I to get your answer."

"Well, you see, it's like this," he said. "I'm in one of them, er, delicate situations. What we have here is a conflict of interests—me not being on what you might call the best of terms with the law. I've got my business interests to protect."

"Just what might your business be, Mr. Valentine?"

"Like you, I'm a specialist," he said. "You want something special—valuablelike—I get it for you. At a price, of course."

"I see," she said. "A burglar. And was this friend of yours, the one who was killed, a burglar too?"

"Nope." He shook his head. "Straight as a die was Tony. One of your lot, as a matter of fact. Private eye. Tony had a small business in the centre of town—a one-room office over a dry cleaner's down a side street off London Road. Someone shoved her off an express train. She broke her neck—died instantly, they reckon."

"She?"

"Antonia Manners. She called herself Tony because it was better for business, she said." He paused. Then, nodding his head, "Nice little thing. Only a kid, really. Bit of a dreamer." His eyes widened. "Had no sense of humour, mind. . . . Got a reputation, I have, for being able to spin a good yarn, but Tony . . ." He shook his head. "She'd just sit listening, and when I'd said my piece, she'd be quiet for a minute, then she'd nod and say, 'Yes, Jimmy, that was very good, very funny.' " He looked at Mrs. Charles sadly. "But never so much as a titter. Took life very seriously. Even my jokes."

"How old was she?"

"Thirty-one." He paused, shrugged. "Never looked much more'n a kid to me."

"Rather an unusual profession for a woman, isn't it?"

"Is it? You tell me," he said.

The clairvoyante made a small gesture with her hand. "Point taken. However, in my case I drifted into this line of work. It was never something I deliberately set out to do."

"I don't really think it was that way with Tony neither. At least that's always been my impression. Tony never discussed business, the cases she was working on. She wasn't much of a talker. For a woman, that is." He hesitated, frowned reflectively. "Except for that once—the day she died. 'Got to see a man about a ghost, Jimmy. . . .' That was what she said to me . . . almost as if I wasn't there and she was talking to herself. Real strange it was. Like it was something important to her and, come hell or high water, she was going to do it. Sends chills up and down my spine every time I think about it. Then the next thing I hear, she's dead. Not a dozen hours later." He hesitated again, his frown deepened. "They reckon she chucked herself off that train. That was what they said at the inquest—the coppers investigating her death and some old Scottish geezer who spotted her in the corridor of the train. He saw her smoking—sort of resigned, he said she seemed to him as she stubbed out the butt. As if she knew it was her last one. He didn't actually see her jump, but he reckons he had a fair idea she was going to. This was after he'd thought about it, of course. We can all be clever dicks afterwards—once we know something has happened —and say we saw it coming, can't we?" Jimmy Valentine spoke bitterly. Then, abruptly, his mood switched to one of resignation, and with a sigh he said, "Seems he was the last person to see her alive."

"Was that the official verdict . . . suicide?"

He nodded.

"There must've been quite a lot more evidence than that of one witness for the coroner to record that particular verdict."

He shrugged. "The coppers dug up some old information from her medical records. Tony had a breakdown a few years back . . . spent quite some time afterwards recuperating in a nursing home. . . ." His voice trailed off.

"Had she tried to take her life before?"

"I don't think so. Nothing like that was said at the inquest." His voice became bitter again. "It's all wrong, you know . . . the way people jump to conclusions the moment they find out a person's had mental treatment. It's like you've committed some crime—*worse.* . . . You carry it round with you wherever you go for the rest of your life. Condemned, that's what you are. Guilty and with no fair trial neither. Just trot out the medical records and that's it. Suicide while of unsound mind. Next case! It's the same attitude that makes it hopeless for blokes like me to turn over a new leaf and go straight. There's always that question mark hanging over your head. Well, here's one person who's not interested in Tony's past track record. I'm giving her the benefit of the doubt."

"And that's all you've really got to go on, your doubt?"

He didn't answer.

"Are you telling me everything you know, Mr. Valentine?"

"The police asked me the same question," he drawled. "Only not quite so politelike. Someone spotted Tony and me chatting together in the Half Moon—the caff next door to Tony's office, where she used to go for a cuppa—and shopped me. All I could tell them was what I've told you. . . . What Tony said to me as I sat down at the table with her. 'Can't stop,' she said. 'I've got to see a man about a ghost, Jimmy.' And with that, up she jumps, pays for her tea, and off she toddles!"

"Perhaps this was merely her polite way of saying she didn't have time to sit about talking."

"Making a joke of it, y'mean?" He shook his head. "Naw, I told you. Tony had no sense of humour. She never joked about anything."

"You also said she never discussed business."

His eyebrows went up. "Did I say it had anything to do with business? The police checked her files, and they couldn't find any link with what she said to me and the cases she was working on. . . . Not that I would've taken their word for it. I checked it out for myself. Soon as I heard she was dead."

"You broke into her office?"

"You are speaking to an artiste, madam. A professional, quite literally to his fingertips, who takes great pride in his work. I did not *break* into Tony's office—no, nothing so crude. I simply unlocked the door—admittedly not quite the same way other folk would—and walked right in."

He suddenly sprang up out of his chair and crossed to the window. Then, clasping his hands behind his back, he stood gazing down the back garden to the wood.

"The police say she was up to her neck in debt—owed money everywhere. Business *was* bad," he admitted after a slight pause. "She only had the one proper case when she died. Just a routine birdnapping. But *I* say she was careful. The files the police and I saw were phoney." He turned abruptly from the window to look at Mrs. Charles and tapped his skull. "The really important stuff she kept up here, in her noggin, where nobody could get at it."

"Did I hear you say a *bird*napping?"

He shrugged, turned, and looked down the garden again. "Hard to tell from the file how big a job it was. A Mrs. Dolly Dackers of Old Memorial Cottage, Uppingham—that was the name and address I saw in the file. The client, I mean. Probably just some little old pensioner who forgot to shut the cage door and thinks someone has pinched her budgie. The rest of the stuff in the filing cabinet was bills, mostly final demands, like the coppers said."

His head shot forward, and he stared intently at something moving near the wire rear fence. "There's a bloke down on all fours at the bottom of your garden. He's crawling through the grass."

"Mr. North," said Mrs. Charles.

"He's waving to someone," said Jimmy Valentine when Stan North suddenly scrambled to his feet and then broke through the long grass and took several steps towards the bungalow.

The hair follicles on the back of Jimmy Valentine's neck prickled. "You've got company," he said. "Can't see his face. Big bloke. Going grey. Walks like a bleedin' copper!"

"That'll be David Sayer," said the clairvoyante.

"There used to be a Sayer over at the Gidding Nick," said

Jimmy Valentine. His head shot round. "Friend of yours?" he asked.

"His aunt lives in that small cottage at the top of the road."

"What's he want here?"

"Why not wait and find out?"

Jimmy Valentine grinned. "You can tell me all about it later." He started for the door. "You'll take the case, won't you?"

"I have a choice?"

"Not really. If you need me you can get hold of me at the Half Moon in town. They'll know where to find me if I'm not around."

"One question before you go, Mr. Valentine. Why? What does it matter to you whether or not a small-time private investigator was murdered?"

Mrs. Charles caught only part of his reply, which floated back over his shoulder as he made a hasty exit. Something about his being sentimental . . .

There was no sign of the man anywhere by the time Mrs. Charles rose to answer the ring of her front doorbell.

"Just thought I'd stop by and make sure everything's okay here," ex-Detective Chief Superintendent David Sayer greeted her. "There have been a number of sightings of a prowler in and around the village today . . . slightly built, weasel-faced chap of between fifty and sixty." (A fair description of Jimmy Valentine, thought the clairvoyante.) "Nobody appears to have been burgled," David went on, "though my aunt was convinced that he'd got off with her antique opera glasses. Which you'll be no doubt sorry to hear I've since found wedged down between the seat cushion and the side of her armchair," he said with a wry smile. Stan North said he spotted a man skulking about near here earlier this afternoon—somewhere around two—and I wondered if he paid you a visit while you were out."

"He may have done," she said. "The back door wasn't locked. I certainly haven't noticed anything missing," she added as they went through to the sitting room to check. "As a matter of fact," she continued, "some of the individual pieces of furniture in here are my most valuable possessions, but he would've needed something a whole lot bigger than a swag bag to carry off this little lot."

"And don't be surprised if some long, dark winter's night he doesn't drop back with a couple of his mates and a van," said David in a dry voice.

"I'll bear it in mind," she said with a smile.

There was a small, somehow expectant pause. Then Mrs. Charles said, "Drink, Superintendent? The usual?"

"Thanks, don't mind if I do," he said, obediently sitting down when she waved him over to a chair.

She poured two straight whiskies before sitting down opposite him.

"How is your aunt?" she inquired.

"Difficult as ever. And you, Madame? It's been quite some time. . . . You've been out the last few times I've called over to see the old lady."

David looked at her searchingly. She wasn't going to tell him anything, he knew the signs. Still, maybe Stan North was mistaken. Maybe it was some other man and not the weasel-faced village prowler he saw outlined against the net curtains of the rear room the clairvoyante used as an office. Maybe that man, whoever he was—a client, perhaps—was waiting for her now out the back, waiting for him to leave.

David swallowed the last of his drink in a gulp and rose. "Well, I'll be running along, Madame. I won't keep you. I'm sure you're busy. Thanks for the drink. You must call in on Jean and me next time you're in Gidding."

"I will, Superintendent," she promised, going with him to the door. Then, as he was about to take his leave, she said, "Oh, before you go . . . There's a name that keeps going round and round in my head—I simply can't get it off my mind—and for some reason I find myself associating it with you." She paused, inclined her head on one side, and regarded him thoughtfully. "Jimmy Valentine . . . Now where have I heard that name before?"

David repeated the name, shook his head. "No one I know. Never heard of him." He hesitated, looking at her closely. "There's the bloke in that old popular song, of course. I'm sure you remember it. I forget now how it went —something about keeping a watch out (or was it a look out?) for Jimmy Valentine. . . ."

"Oh yes," she said with a slow nod. "The sentimental crook. I remember. . . ."

CHAPTER TWO

"It's a hoax," pronounced the clairvoyante's brother, Cyril Forbes, his tone implying that, so far as he was concerned, the subject was closed. "Forget it," he said, glancing up from a copy of the outer space magazine he published.

His sister, rising, crossed to the door of his paper-cluttered study, where she paused with her hand on the knob. "I only wish I could, Cyril," she said. "Unfortunately, I can't."

"Because of Edwin?"

She nodded absently.

"Look," he said, reluctantly putting aside the magazine. "For once I agree with Sayer. That fellow's going to come back some night with a great big van and clean up in the village. You told me he said he was good at spinning a tale, and that's all he was doing. You caught him out, in the act of going through your place, so he made up that story about the private eye. Edwin and he obviously spent some time together in prison. And you don't need me to remind you what Edwin was like once he got started, what a big mouth he had. He talked about you, told this fellow Valentine what you do, where you live—it sticks out a mile, Dell!—and Valentine reckoned he might be onto a good thing if he dropped over here sometime and paid us all a visit."

"I told you, Cyril. He was waiting for me out in the road. In broad daylight and in full view of everyone."

"But according to what you said a while ago, North told Sayer he saw the fellow hanging about your place earlier in the day, around lunchtime."

"Exactly." She nodded. "And that's why I say he really came to the village to see me. He simply filled in the time while waiting for me to come home by doing what comes naturally to him."

Cyril sighed. "So what are you going to do about it?"

She thought for a moment. "Well, it seems to me that the only thing to do is to tackle the story he told me. If that proves to be false, then that will be it. I'll accept David Sayer's theory and change the locks on all my doors and windows."

Cyril got up and followed his sister to the front door. "Where are you going to start?"

"Where his story was set, Cyril. In a small, one-room office over a dry cleaner's in Gidding . . ."

Soon after ten the following morning, Mrs. Charles and Cyril (he had insisted on accompanying his sister ". . . to stop you doing anything silly," he had told her) walked slowly down Mallard Lane, a short, narrow, dead-end street off the main road through Gidding's busy shopping centre.

Halfway down the lane, Mrs. Charles paused and looked across the road at the blue and white plastic sign over the Half Moon Cafe. An estate agent's board jutted out from a dirty window on the first floor of the building next door; the ground floor was wholly taken up by a dry cleaner's.

"Coincidence," said Cyril, looking up and seeing the OF-FICE TO LET sign. He looked round quickly when there was no reply. His sister was walking back up the lane, and he guessed where she was going.

The junior negotiator who accompanied Mrs. Charles and her brother from the offices of Hammond & Co. round the corner in London Road made a sweeping gesture with his right arm as he showed his prospective clients into the tiny, dingy office they had asked to see and assured them that a firm of office cleaners had been contracted to come in and clean up the place. In fact, he said, he was rather surprised the job hadn't already been done: he'd get onto the contractors as soon as he got back to the office.

He was a very young man, still a little unsure of himself and therefore inclined to be talkative. He watched Mrs. Charles out of the corner of an eye. Yes, he had a punter there, all right: she was definitely interested. But the weird little guy with her wasn't.

"You said you're looking for suitable premises for a magazine you publish?" remarked the young man when his other stock conversational pieces began to dry up.

"It's my brother's magazine, not mine," replied Mrs. Charles, indicating her head in the direction of Cyril, who had wandered off, thereby justifying the young man's pessimism over the likelihood of negotiating a deal with him.

Mrs. Charles inched some dusty sheets of typing paper along the floor with the toe of her shoe. "It rather looks as if the last tenant left in something of a hurry," she observed.

"Oh, don't take any notice of this mess," he said. He swiftly gathered up the pieces of paper from the floor, looked round for a wastepaper bin, then left them on the grimy windowsill. "It was the police who left the place like this when they cleared everything out. The previous tenant committed suicide," he explained. "Not here, on the premises," he put in quickly. "In fact, she jumped off an express train. Miles from here," he added to be on the safe side. "She'd got herself into one hell of a mess."

Mrs. Charles looked at him questioningly, and he considered the possibility that he might be talking too much. He had done that in his previous position with a timber importer and then, just as the client was about to sign, insisted on jumping on the sample piece of merchandise to prove how tough it was. The plank of wood had splintered, whereupon the customer had immediately cancelled his order and the young trainee salesman found himself out of a job.

The young man frowned a little and played it safe. "Personal problems, I think," he said. "I'm not really sure."

The office was empty of furniture save for an old desk and a broken kitchen chair near the window. Mrs. Charles went over to the desk and opened a drawer. But for a heavy coating of dust and a collection of thick fluff in the corners, both it and the drawer beneath it, when Mrs. Charles looked in that one too, were empty.

"Don't worry about the desk," said the young man quickly. "We'll soon have that old junk taken away."

"How long have the premises been empty?"

Ah, thought the young man. She's heard about the fumes from the cleaner's downstairs.

"Oh, not long," he said vaguely. "About two months. We—that is, Mr. Hammond—couldn't do much about reletting the place until everything was straightened out about Miss Manners—the previous tenant . . . the woman who killed herself."

Mrs. Charles nodded. "I see. Are there likely to be any problems with the Council?"

He gave her a startled look. "No, I wouldn't think so. I mean, er, in what way?"

"The Council won't object to the premises being used as the registered office of a magazine?"

"Well, er . . . ." The young negotiator hesitated. "I'm not sure about that. I don't think so. You'd have to have a word with Mr. Hammond there. Mr. Hammond owns the building, of course." The young man made this admission reluctantly, as if he thought it was wiser not to part with this particular piece of information. "I mean, I don't know about the Council, but I don't think Mr. Hammond would want to see the premises used for anything . . . er, well, you know . . . *immoral.* That is"—he frowned—*"pornographic.* He was never too happy about Miss Manners's line of business—" The young man winced. He had a feeling he'd done it again, jumped on the plank of wood.

"What line of business was she in?"

The young man was tempted to say Miss Manners ran an employment agency but guessed that his prospective client was shrewd enough to make her own inquiries (if it were that important to her to know) and opted for the truth.

"She was a private inquiry agent," he answered. "Only

very small-time, of course. Most people would want a man to handle that sort of thing for them, wouldn't they? Someone a bit older, anyway . . . more mature. Miss Manners couldn't have been much more than thirty. She wasn't the kind of person . . . well, I don't know." He shrugged. "I found it hard to take her seriously. And there was nothing to her. Though I daresay she had some muscle-bound male who made sure she came to no harm. Some of these divorce cases can get pretty hairy, can't they? But I don't think you'd have anything to worry about. . . . I mean, er, if you thought some irate ex-husband was going to come up here and mistake you for Miss Manners. Mr. Hammond said the police went through her files, and they told him she only had one client when she died. She filled in most of her time—this was when she wasn't next door in the Half Moon—with part-time work as a store detective."

"She sounds as though she had a hard time of it," commented Mrs. Charles, moving towards the door where Cyril, behind the negotiator's back, was signalling to her to hurry up.

"I guess she did," admitted the young man. "But then she really ought to have had more sense, in my opinion, and grown up. That sort of thing's strictly for T.V. Whoever's heard of a female P.I. in real life?"

Mrs. Charles raised her eyebrows a bit but made no comment. He locked the door behind them: then, catching up with Mrs. Charles, who had gone on ahead, he said, "Look . . . er, well, if you think you could be interested . . . I mean . . . well, er, I daresay we could get Mrs. Flegg to pop round and give the place a thorough clean for you. Instead of waiting for the contractors to come, that is. Mrs. Flegg takes care of our holiday lets for us. I'm sure she wouldn't mind. She often fitted in an hour here and there for Miss Manners."

He looked at the time. "Mrs. Flegg won't be in at the moment, she's out most of the day. And unfortunately she's not on the phone. But I could drop round and see her tonight on my way home from the office, if you'd like. She only lives round the corner . . . in that high-rise block of Council flats off the new shopping precinct. It'd be no trouble. I mean, er, if you *really* think you'd be interested."

Cyril's bullet-shaped head suddenly shot round the newel post at the top of the stairs.

"What's that funny smell?" he demanded.

Hammond & Co.'s negotiator contrived to look innocent. "Smell? I can't smell anything."

"Then it's probably already too late for you," said Cyril. He looked at his sister. "If you're serious about this place, you'd better see there's a clause in the tenancy agreement covering us for compensation for brain damage caused by the inhalation of fumes from dry cleaning fluid."

Mrs. Charles turned to the young negotiator and looked at him thoughtfully. "How long was Miss Manners a tenant?"

Colour suffused his acne-scarred face. "It wasn't that," he said. "What you're thinking. I mean, er, they went into that thoroughly at the inquest. Mr. Hammond was very relieved when they said there was no evidence of brain damage as a result of the faulty ventilation downstairs. . . ."

Crunch! If he hadn't jumped on the plank before, then the young man knew for certain he had now.

As they sat at a small table in the window of the Half Moon Cafe drinking tea, Cyril expounded his theories on the harmful effects of constant exposure to dry cleaning fumes. He was amazed that his sister hadn't noticed the overpowering smell. "It's why Tony Manners spent so much of her time in here," he explained.

"How do you know that?" asked his sister.

"*She* told me . . . Jill over there." He nodded his head at the counter, where a pretty teenager in a dark blue overall leaned on her folded arms gazing dreamily out of the window.

He went on, "While you were upstairs with chummy . . . Jill reckons Tony just about used this place as her office because the fumes gave her such bad headaches and made her feel depressed all the time."

The girl leaning on the counter suddenly looked their way and gave Cyril a shy smile.

Mrs. Charles regarded her brother contemplatively. She had always known that despite his unfortunate looks, his remarkable likeness to Punch—the principal figure in the puppet show he put on for children—women found him irresistible, but hitherto she had assumed it was only late–middle-aged matrons who succumbed to his charms. There was obviously a great deal more to Cyril than met the eye— far more than she would ever have supposed, she admitted to herself with a small smile.

"Perhaps," she said slowly, "it was not so much that, the fumes, as a lack of work that made her headachy and depressed."

Cyril did not argue. He chose a fresh line of attack. "Mrs. Wong—the owner of this place—said your friend Valentine was making a nuisance of himself with the Manners girl."

Mrs. Charles gave her brother a sharp look. The cafe proprietress too had fallen under his spell? And in so short a time?

Cyril went on, "That's what Jill told me. Mrs. Wong reckons the Manners girl spotted him heading her way that morning and that this was why she folded up her newspaper and cleared off. She'd only just sat down too. Hadn't even touched her tea."

"Maybe she was following somebody?"

Cyril gazed wide-eyed about him at the empty tables and chairs and the deserted lane beyond. "Jill said they only get the odd customer or two until the lunchtime office crowd comes in around noon, and that morning there was no one in here but her and Mrs. Wong and Tony Manners until Valentine showed up."

"This Mrs. Wong knows him—Jimmy Valentine—by that name?"

He shrugged. "Never thought to ask. Jill just called him 'Jimmy.' "

Cyril was silent for a minute. "You know what I think, Del," he said. "I think he fancied Tony Manners and weaving some fanciful tale around the way she died, makes him feel better."

His sister merely shook her head at his questioning look.

"I don't honestly see that there's anything more you can do, Del," he said. "The girl committed suicide, it's up to you to convince Valentine of it. That shouldn't be difficult. You're good at getting people to face up to facts."

"I daresay you're right," she sighed.

Cyril looked at her closely. He didn't like that faraway look in her eye.

"You've not got one of your funny feelings about this, have you?"

"No," she said. "It's just rather sad, that's all. I think that poor girl must've had a tough time of it."

"Being sorry for someone won't alter the facts."

"No, Cyril. That's the one thing we can be sure of."

CHAPTER THREE

The man screwed up his eyes and grunted as he reached down to lift the crate of light ale off the cellar floor. The pain in his chest was bad this morning. He paused, frowning to himself. Well, what was he supposed to do? Get the girl to hump this heavy lot about?

He cursed under his breath. Over three million unemployed and yet nobody wanted to work. The employment office had even given up sending people round. . . .

The man rested for a minute on one of the concrete cellar steps.

MacDonald warned him that the next heart attack would probably be his last, that he should give up the pub, find something less strenuous. . . .

But it wasn't the hard work that was killing him. Hard work never hurt anybody, the man assured himself. It was all this worry about staff, getting more help in the bar—like a reliable cellarman . . . first finding someone and then keeping that person.

And then, right on top of everything else, this other business . . .

But that was life, everything bearing down on you all at once.

He closed his eyes and gently massaged his forehead with the thick fingertips of his large, clumsy-looking hands.

Two months since the girl fell off that train, and nobody had made the connection. They wouldn't now; too much time had elapsed.

He tried to analyse how he felt about that. He thought he should feel pleased, and yet somehow he wasn't—probably because of her, the girl. She'd been as involved as the others, there was no denying that, but with her it had been different. People could argue all they liked that the others too had only been doing their job, but right from the beginning, they'd been out for blood. Specially that copper. He was the worst of the lot. A proper bastard.

A strange look—a curious mixture of pleasure and satisfaction—crossed the man's broad, flat face. They couldn't say they hadn't been warned. They should've known it was no idle threat and that one day every man Jack of them would be made to pay for what they'd done. And that made it two down (three if you counted the girl), one to go. . . . "Or my name's not Roger M. Purdie," the man murmured to himself with a sly, wolfish grin.

"Dad! Are you down there?"

The man gave a start, then looked up guiltily as his stepdaughter, Ellen, started down the cellar steps. She hesitated when she saw the ashen pallor of his cheeks, the tiny beads of sweat on his brow.

"Are you feeling all right?" she asked. "I'll give you a hand with that crate."

"No. You get back up there where you belong," he snapped. "It's time we were opening up, anyway."

"It's early," she said. "It's only five to eleven."

"You heard what I said," he growled. "When I need your help I'll ask for it."

The girl shrugged, then started back up the steps. These sudden switches of mood of his confused her. But at least she understood what her mother had meant when she had insisted that he wasn't the man she had married. There were days just lately when Ellen didn't know him any more either. He seemed like a complete stranger to her.

David Sayer was out when the clairvoyante called to see him at his home in Gidding around three that afternoon. She was alone. Cyril, once she had acquainted him with her plans (and anxious not to compromise his position with the ex-detective chief superintendent of police with whom he still felt aggrieved over their past differences of opinion), had elected to return home when they had parted earlier in the day outside the Half Moon.

David finally put in an appearance as Mrs. Charles and David's vivacious wife, Jean, were having afternoon tea. It took a while, but the steady stare under raised eyebrows which he directed every so often his wife's way eventually conveyed to her his expectation that the clairvoyante's visits was unlikely to be a purely social one.

Slightly flustered, Jean abruptly got up and began to clear away the tea things. She was unable to keep her dismay out of her voice when the clairvoyante also rose.

"Oh," said Jean. "You're not leaving already, are you? I didn't mean to hurry you. I just thought—" She paused, gave her husband a look, a silent plea for help, which he steadfastly ignored. "What I mean is," Jean went on with a mutinous glare at her immovable spouse, "I'm sure there are things you'd both like to talk about. . . . In private, that is," she added, addressing herself now to Mrs. Charles.

The clairvoyante, who was gazing idly out of the window, appeared not to have heard. Then, looking at Jean, she smiled and said, "I must confess that I did think I might take the opportunity of discussing something with you while I was in Gidding today, but I've since decided that I'm really being very silly, making a mountain out of something that isn't even a molehill."

"Oh," said Jean in a very small voice. The forlorn look she gave the clairvoyante betrayed her disappointment that neither she nor her husband were, it seemed, to be made privy to whatever was on their visitor's mind.

David regarded Mrs. Charles thoughtfully.

"That doesn't sound much like you," he remarked.

"No," she agreed. "It's most unusual for me to concern myself needlessly, and I'm not at all sure I know why I feel as I do." Her gaze strayed to the window again. "Out of pity, I think. Though I don't really know for whom, her or him—

the man who asked me to find the girl's killer. I'm afraid it's as Cyril said—I should really be applying myself now to the problem of how to convince this man, my client, that his killer is nothing more than a figment of his imagination."

"Were they lovers or something?" asked Jean, sitting down again and clasping her hands round her knees.

"I hardly think so. I'm not sure what their relationship was. There were quite a few blanks in the information I was given, both about my client and the girl."

"Who was she? Or mustn't I ask a direct question like that?" Jean put in quickly with a wide-eyed look at her husband.

"No, by all means, ask away!" said Mrs. Charles, smiling at her. "It was a young woman named Antonia, Tony Manners."

David was surprised to see his wife nod and even more surprised when she said, "I read about her in the *Sketch*." Jean looked at her husband. "It was while you were up in Scotland a couple of months ago checking on those lorry hijackings for the whisky distillers. Tony Manners was a private inquiry agent. Or she liked to think she was—isn't that right?" she asked Mrs. Charles, who nodded. Jean went on, "She lived in a bit of a fantasy world, as near as I could make out. Fancied herself as something of a female Philip Marlowe. Then all of a sudden she came down to earth with an awful jolt when her doctor told her she was almost certainly going to finish up like her father, a helpless invalid, bedridden. Apparently she'd always been haunted by the fear that this was going to happen to her too." Jean paused, narrowed her eyes. "I forget now what he had wrong with him. Some progressive muscle-wasting disease, I think. Anyway, she—Tony Manners—went to see a faith healer about it, he obviously couldn't do anything for her either, so in a fit of depression she threw herself off a train one night and was killed instantly."

David looked at Mrs. Charles for confirmation and she nodded. To Jean, she said, "It's odd that you should say Tony was haunted by her fear over her father's physical condition. She made a similar remark to my client the last time he saw her—which, incidentally, he claims was the morning of the day she died. She told him she was going to see a man about a ghost." Mrs. Charles thought for a moment. Then she asked, "Have you any idea if her father is still alive?"

"I think I can remember reading that he died about a year ago," said Jean.

"So it could've been her father's ghost she was talking about," said the clairvoyante with a thoughtful nod. "Would you happen to know who the faith healer was?"

"Mr. Bing. He's quite well-known . . . got a very good reputation." Jean broke off with a small, embarrassed laugh. "At least that was what it said in the *Sketch*. His name usually crops up somewhere on that page near the back of the *Sketch* where they give all the information about local church services and the days for healing at the Spiritualist Church."

"Yes, I've heard of him," said Mrs. Charles. "The Spiritualist Church in Lymstead, isn't it?"

"There's one here in Gidding now," said Jean. "They started one up about two or three months ago. A sort of sister church to the one in Lymstead, and Mr. Bing floats back and forth between the two."

Mrs. Charles smiled at the expectant way David was looking at her.

"No, I'm afraid not, Superintendent. I know nothing but good about Benjamin Bing."

Mrs. Charles sat quietly thinking in a shady corner of the bus shelter. David had offered to drive her back to the village, but she had declined on the pretext that she had some shopping still to do in the town. She had really wanted to meditate on the events of the day and then dismiss the whole matter of Tony Manners's tragic death from her mind. The twenty-five-mile, ponderously slow bus journey back home to the village of Little Gidding would give her that opportunity.

Her thoughts centred mainly on the man who called himself Jimmy Valentine and his true motives for seeking her out. Was she (thanks to Edwin) merely just another victim to him—someone it might possibly be worthwhile visiting late one night with a jemmy and a sack? Or was he the sentimental crook he claimed to be—a man whose path had somehow crossed that of the young private inquiry agent's? Maybe Cryil was right (he could often be astonishingly perceptive about people and their motives): maybe Jimmy Valentine had been smitten with the girl and then, unable to come to terms with his grief over her death, he had invented a story of murder because it was more acceptable than to have to acknowledge that she had taken her own life.

It wasn't the clairvoyante's impression that he was guilty about something. A man like Jimmy Valentine had no conscience—he was a pathological crook and was perfectly contented with his lot.

Mrs. Charles averted her head and closed her eyes against the hot, dry wind which had sprung up since lunchtime and which blew in short, swirling, dust-laden gusts. It had started out a pleasantly warm, sunny August day, but somewhere around noon the temperature had begun a steady climb into the low eighties and at a few minutes after four this was the hottest time of day. She blinked quickly to clear the dust and grit from her eyes, then concentrated on her problem.

The main difficulty was going to be convincing Jimmy Valentine that his young lady friend had committed suicide. Mrs. Charles frowned a little. Just how big a threat was he to her (this was supposing he refused to believe that she had looked into the girl's death for him)? How much had Edwin told him? Fortunately for her, she thought wryly, the most prominent client—the M.P.—who dated back to the depressing days of the Charles the Third period had since died. But there were still enough names, names of some very important people socially and politically, the publication of which could place them (and her) in very hot water.

There was no doubt about it, Edwin had been a mistake. A bad one.

The urgent whisperings of two young voices intruded on the clairvoyante's thoughts, and she looked round slowly. A girl and boy of about seventeen or eighteen stood close together at the far end of the long, narrow bus shelter.

The girl said, "I can't. Dad'll kill me if I'm not back before opening time. You know what he's like. It'll be bad enough if he finds out where I've been this afternoon. He'll know I've been with you, anyway. You can't keep anything from him for long."

The boy scowled. "Tell the old goat to get knotted. He just uses you. You're nothing but cheap labour to him. It's not even as if he's your real father."

"I told you," the girl protested. "He's been trying for ages to get help."

"Oh yeah, I bet!"

Abruptly, the girl stepped away from him and onto the roadway and gazed into the distance. "A bus is coming," she said after a moment.

"You'll think about what I said—that other business—and come down to London with me? You'll be all right there. He'll never find us, I promise you."

"And what are we going to do for money?" she asked.

"Listen . . . I told you how we can take care of that. It'll be easy, no danger. We'll be miles from here by the time he realises the money's missing."

"It's all right for you to say that," she hissed. "What if he checks the safe? He does some nights."

"Okay, so we don't wait for morning, we'll clear off straight away—as soon as you've cleaned the cash out of the till and gone through to the back to count it. You slip away while he's locking up. I'll be waiting outside for you. We'll thumb a ride down to London. Don't be a mug, Ellen. He owes you for all the hours you put in. What d'you say?"

The girl said, "No." She sounded scared. "He'll find us, I know he will. He never lets anybody get the better of him. You don't know him like I do. He'll follow us to the ends of the earth to get his money back. I don't want to have anything to do with it."

"All right, I'll take care of it all by myself. Tonight when he calls time and tells you to lock the front door, you forget the bolts and see that the door is left on the latch. Just leave the money in the till and go straight upstairs and pack some things. I'll see to everything else."

"*No*, Trev!" The girl signed to the bus driver with her outstretched arm and the bus—the one for Lymstead—pulled in at the shelter, and she moved forward and boarded it.

"Tonight," he called out as the bus pulled away. "I'm counting on you."

The last Mrs. Charles saw of the girl she was vigorously shaking her head.

Scowling, the boy stood for a moment watching the back of the vanishing bus and then, with a startled exclamation, he suddenly swung round. Two youths, friends of his, who had apparently been observing him from some concealed spot, swooped down on him and began chaffing him about his girlfriend. There was a lot of coarse laughter and some ribald comment which ceased abruptly when two teenaged girls on the other side of the road called loudly across to one of them.

"You'd better get off home sharpish, Trevor Flegg. Your mother's looking for you, and she isn't half mad!"

Trevor Flegg, the boy who had been under attack from his friends, made one or two impolite suggestions to the girls, who stuck their noses in the air and pretended indifference. As they began to saunter away, all three boys crossed the road and followed them, catcalling to them and mimicking their hobbled walk (both girls wore identical tight, black leather miniskirts and shoes with exaggerated high heels and flimsy ankle straps).

Flegg, thought the clairvoyante, as she watched their progress down the road. It was an unusual name. Not the kind one would expect to hear twice in the same day.

Without consciously thinking about what she was doing, Mrs. Charles rose and left the bus shelter, then made her way back into the town centre.

CHAPTER FOUR

The elderly caretaker at the block of flats could not have been more helpful. Not that this meant he had done a turn-about and now approved of social workers (a sharp dose of army training was the only way to straighten out the likes of the Flegg boy, and the sooner the better in the old man's opinion); but at least this new one wasn't the long-haired trendy subversive he usually came up against. No, thought the old man, as he prepared to give Edwina Charles directions to the Fleggs' flat, this smartly turned-out woman was a great improvement. The type, he thought, who would stand for no nonsense and mean what she said.

He gave Mrs. Charles the information she sought and then, when she had finished thanking him, informed her that Mrs. Flegg was in: she had got back from work half an hour ago, he said. However, he added, he hadn't laid eyes on Trevor since first thing this morning. "That was if you were thinking of having a word with him too," he finished on a hopeful note.

"No, it's Mrs. Flegg I want to see, thank you," said Mrs. Charles.

The old man nodded sympathetically. Poor Mrs. Flegg, he thought, watching Mrs. Charles walk away. That lad of hers would be the death of somebody yet—that somebody, in the caretaker's view (and he pictured the scene vividly), being some poor old pensioner living on her own and brutally done to death for her savings.

The door of flat number 8 was opened by a small, spare woman in her middle forties. She wasn't a pretty woman, but her face was friendly and kind.

"Good afternoon," said the clairvoyante. "Mrs. Flegg?"

The woman nodded.

"A young gentleman from Hammond & Co., the estate agents in London Road, suggested that you might be able to help me," Mrs. Charles went on. "I wonder if I could possibly have a word with you about Miss Manners—Tony?"

Mrs. Flegg's face saddened. "Ah yes, the poor wee thing." She spoke with a thick Scottish accent.

"I understand you occasionally worked for her," said Mrs. Charles.

"Only charring," said Mrs. Flegg. "And actually it was quite often—on a regular basis once a week. It was only occasionally that the poor girl could afford to pay me. 'Enid,' she used to say to me"—Mrs. Flegg's voice softened reminiscently, her grey eyes clouded—" 'If I can only just hang on a little bit longer, I know my luck will change. It's sure to turn soon,' she said."

Several small children came out of the flat next door and began to play noisily in the long, cheerless corridor.

"You'd better come in," said Mrs. Flegg as the children's voices reached screaming pitch. "We'll not be able to hear ourselves think out here."

Mrs. Charles stepped straight into a neat, economically furnished living room. The Fleggs were clearly not well-off. And Mrs. Flegg, the clairvoyante strongly suspected, probably earned most of whatever little money went into the family exchequer each week. She had the look about her of a good, honest, hardworking woman. (And one who would unfortunately appear to be afflicted with a ne'er-do-well son, who seemed destined to bring her nothing but grief.)

The clairvoyante returned the solemn gaze of the albino cockatiel perched in its cage near the window before accepting Mrs. Flegg's invitation to be seated. Then she said, "My name is Edwina Charles. I've been hired to look into Tony's death."

Mrs. Flegg looked surprised. "I thought it was all over and

done with. Tony committed suicide. That was what the coroner said at the inquest."

"You knew her personally, Mrs. Flegg. What do you say? Would you have thought Tony was the kind of person to commit suicide?"

Mrs. Flegg seemed taken aback by the question. "I—I don't know. . . ." She hesitated, her eyes widened. "Well, didn't she?"

"Yes, probably. But I must be sure."

Mrs. Flegg looked hard at her visitor. She spoke hesitantly. "You say somebody *hired* you? I didn't think Tony had any family. She never spoke of anyone. . . . I mean, after her old dad passed on."

"The man for whom I am working was a close friend."

"Oh, I see," said Mrs. Flegg, and nodded as if that explained everything.

"May I ask if you were surprised that Tony had taken her own life?"

Mrs. Flegg thought for a minute. "No. I knew she was worried about it—that complaint her dad had. She mentioned it a couple of times—this was when he was still alive —and said she expected she'd get it one day. She made it sound as if she was resigned, but she wasn't, not really. Well, you couldn't be, could you? Not to something like that. It's only natural you'd always be hoping that somebody'd come up with a cure, isn't it?"

"Did you know that Tony consulted Mr. Bing, the faith healer?"

"Yes, but she only saw him the once, the day she died. He felt dreadful about it, poor man. Terribly upset he was at the inquest. All quivering and shaking and practically in tears most of the time. He had to sit down soon after he started giving his evidence and wait while they fetched him a glass of water. A man like him, though—fey, they'd call him where I come from in Scotland—is bound to be sensitive and highly strung, isn't he?"

Mrs. Charles made no comment. "He confirmed that Tony

had consulted him on the day she died about this hereditary condition she feared would be passed on from her father?"

"Yes." Mrs. Flegg nodded. "The poor man was terribly emotional about it, could hardly get his words out." She hesitated, frowned. "I honestly can't imagine why anyone should think there might be something—well, something not quite right about Tony's death. It was obvious that the poor girl was at the end of her tether, what with her poor old dad—caring for him the way she did for all those years—and then all her financial worries on top of it. And it wasn't all that long since he'd died, you know. I'm sure she wasn't properly over it."

Mrs. Charles nodded. "I'm inclined to agree with you, Mrs. Flegg. However, my client—Tony's friend—is most insistent that I should make absolutely sure there was no other reason for her death."

"It sounds to me as if your client loved her very much," observed Mrs. Flegg.

"I rather think so," agreed the clairvoyante. Then, after a small pause, "Just to put my mind completely at rest that I haven't overlooked anything, did Tony say anything to you —or in any way behave in an unusual or odd manner—say, in the last week or two before she died?"

Mrs. Flegg shook her head. "Tony wasn't much of a talker. She was a listener."

"Nothing at all out of the ordinary happened that you can think of?"

Again Mrs. Flegg shook her head. "Everything was the same as always the last time I saw her. I cleaned through, chattering away nineteen to the dozen as usual, and Tony sat and listened."

Mrs. Charles frowned. She was floundering now and she knew it, asking questions which she knew instinctively would lead her nowhere because the answer always would be no.

"Did Tony employ anyone in the office, a typist?"

Mrs. Flegg shook her head.

"Perhaps she occasionally hired some temporary office staff?"

Mrs. Flegg was still shaking her head.

"Tony did everything herself?"

"I never saw her doing any paperwork," said Mrs. Flegg. "There used to be a typewriter about the place at one time, but that suddenly disappeared, went the way of everything else, I expect—down the secondhand shop. When I first started there, the office was quite smart . . . nice furniture —a comfortable sofa for clients to sit on while they waited— one of those posh electric typewriters . . . Then after a while, each time I went, there'd be something else missing. In the finish, there was only the desk, an old chair, the filing cabinet, and the telephone—and they were threatening to come and take that away too."

Mrs. Flegg heaved a sigh. "Sad it was. But never one word of complaint. That was what I liked most about Tony. She never whined and moaned the way some people do when they're down on their luck. Never once did I hear her blame anybody but herself for the mess she was in."

"She blamed herself for being a poor business woman?"

"No, just for being a woman. But she'd always say it with a little smile. It was her way of poking a bit of gentle fun at herself, I always thought."

"Would you have any idea how competent she was at her job?" Mrs. Charles hesitated. Then, inclining her head contemplatively on one side, "Would you, for example, have gone to her if you were in trouble and needed help?"

Mrs. Flegg thought about it. "Yes, I think so. But then again, to be honest with you, that's only because I knew Tony personally. She was the kind of person you felt comfortable with—do you know what I mean? You could tell her things, pour your heart out, and know it'd go no further and that neither would she think any the less of you for it. But if someone had suggested going to a private inquiry agent—I mean, a woman . . . before I got to know Tony, that is . . ." Mrs. Flegg's voice tailed off into a regretful silence.

Then, after a moment, "I daresay you come up against the same sort of prejudice, being a woman and all."

Mrs. Charles smiled noncommittally. Then she asked, "Did you ever overhear Tony talking on the phone to anyone?"

"No. Not for a couple of months before she died, anyway. She hadn't paid the bill. She could only take incoming calls, and there weren't many of them. That was the problem," said Mrs. Flegg in a rueful voice. "But before, when her dad was alive, she only seemed to use it (at least when I was around) to phone her landlady and make sure he was all right. Her landlady used to pop upstairs every now and again to check on him."

They fell silent. There was only one other question the clairvoyante could think to ask, and she didn't really expect it would lead anywhere, simply because, like Jimmy Valentine, she doubted the existence of the woman. The name and address were phoney. There was certainly no Dolly Dackers—no Dackers at all—listed in the telephone directory which covered Uppingham, a small village in a neighbouring county roughly ten miles as the crow flies from Mrs. Charles's own village of Little Gidding.

"Does the name Dackers—Dolly Dackers—mean anything to you?"

Mrs. Flegg looked vaguely embarrassed. "I . . ." She faltered, frowned. "It's a bit awkward. I feel as if I'd be talking out of turn. . . . It was really none of my business— Tony never even knew I was there—and I certainly wasn't going to embarrass her by mentioning that I'd been in the shop when he told her off."

Mrs. Flegg hesitated, looked at Mrs. Charles, perhaps waiting for some word of encouragement to continue with her thus far disjointed narrative. When the clairvoyante remained silent, Mrs. Flegg reluctantly went on.

"But then again, if you think it might be important . . . That—Dackers—was the girl's name, the sixteen-year-old who ran off to Gretna Green with Neville Krendel—the man who runs that pet shop in the shopping precinct. You must've passed it on your way here," she said, and Mrs. Charles nodded.

Mrs. Flegg continued. "It was all over the front page of the *Sketch* some time back now about how Mr. Krendel used to be the girl's mum's lover. He worked for Mrs. Dackers as a bird keeper until they had some kind of argument over the way he was doing his job—or wasn't doing it—and he walked out on her. I'm not sure what she's doing now (since the trouble with Mr. Krendel and her daughter, I mean), but Mrs. Dackers used to breed small cage birds, won ever so many first prizes for her birds, it said in the *Sketch*. But as I was saying about Mr. Krendel and her daughter . . . After he walked out on Mrs. Dackers, her daughter suddenly up and disappeared, and Mrs. Dackers called in the police. Then blow me down if the girl and Mr. Krendel don't turn themselves in to the first police station they came to—this was somewhere near to Gretna Green where they were honeymooning—and bold as brass admit who they were and that they were married. All legal-like. Mrs. Dackers made a terrible fuss about it—said some dreadful things about her daughter and Mr. Krendel to the newspaper people. I don't honestly know how a mother could do such a terrible thing. Very bitter she was. . . . Especially about the money. Well, you'd know there'd be money involved, wouldn't you?" Mrs. Flegg made a wry face. "The girl's dad left her quite a bit of money. It was one of those unusual wills. . . . The way I understood it, her mum had complete control of everything until she reached twenty-one or got married, whichever came first."

"Are you telling me that Tony was carrying out some kind of private investigation for Mrs. Dackers in connection with this man and her daughter?"

Mrs. Flegg replied hesitantly.

"I don't know for sure, you understand, but I was in the pet shop one day buying some sunflower seed for Chippie— my lad's cockatiel over there in the cage"—she nodded her head at it—"when Tony suddenly came in with Mrs. Laffont's toy poodle (Mrs. Laffont was Tony's landlady). I was at the other end of the shop hidden behind some tall shelves and Tony didn't see me, thank heavens—and Mr. Krendel was ever so rude to her about Mrs. Laffont's dog. He won't have them in his shop at any price—says they upset the birds, but it's him they upset. He really hates them. I've heard him before telling customers off for ignoring his ban on bringing their dogs into the shop with them. Anyway, the moment he started going hammer and tongs at Tony about it, I sort of made myself as small and inconspicuous as I could. I didn't want to embarrass her any more than she was already. Really nasty he was to her. Understandable, I suppose. . . . I mean, if he was onto her and he knew she was really keeping watch on him for the girl's mother."

"That was how it looked to you?"

Mrs. Flegg considered the question, shrugged. "Well, that's what they do, isn't it? Tail people? It certainly seemed that way to me . . . that she'd borrowed Mrs. Laffont's dog and used it as a good excuse for getting a closer look at Mr. Krendel. But—well, I suppose it could've been a coincidence. Though I must say it didn't seem that way to me at the time."

Mrs. Charles nodded thoughtfully. A *bird*napping, Jimmy Valentine had said. She had taken him literally, but perhaps the "bird" was actually Mrs. Dackers's sixteen-year-old daughter. . . .

Mrs. Flegg went on, "Lord knows what that silly young girl—Mrs. Dackers's daughter—sees in that dreadful man. I don't think I've met a nastier person. One of these superior types who think they know it all. I hate going into his shop. But . . ." she sighed. "It's convenient and you know how it is. . . . You have a look at the place when you go by. He must have a fortune tied up in those birds he's got hanging up in cages in his window."

Mrs. Charles took Mrs. Flegg's advice and paused outside the Birdarama in the shopping precinct as she made her way past a short while later. She had observed the main window display of exotic parrots and cockatoos while on her way to see Mrs. Flegg and was therefore more interested this time in the various signs in the windows. She noted that the author of the signs, which were mostly handwritten, had a problem with the possessive case: all words ending with an *s* were accorded an apostrophe. She further noted that Mr. Krendel's dislike of dogs did not extend to the sale of canine requisites. Every conceivable luxury item imaginable plus an extensive range of tinned dog food, artistically displayed in a skilfully built-up pyramid, completely filled one of the smaller side windows. The sign which Tony Manners, for reasons best known to herself, had chosen to ignore read . . .

NO PETS' ALLOWED.

ALL DOGS' MUST

REMAIN OUTSIDE.

Beside this sign was a piece of white card on which someone had drawn a thick black outline of a dog's head and then cancelled it out with an oblique red line.

A sulphur-crested cockatoo regarded Mrs. Charles quizzically through the bars of its cage. Spying him, she smiled whimsically to herself and wondered if young Master Flegg intended to take his cockatiel with him when he headed for London. *If* he headed for London . . . And that, thought the clairvoyante as she made her way to the nearest taxi rank, rather depended on how successful he was tonight, his first and possibly biggest obstacle being whether or not his young girlfriend would leave the relevant door on the latch for him.

CHAPTER FIVE

David Sayer looked at the time. It was almost two, coming dangerously close to that hour of the day when his aunt, provided she had no other plans for the afternoon, would return from the Day Centre and take up her position in the bay window. With her binoculars, of course. And that was the last thing he wanted . . . for her to get wind of what was in the air. Or rather, what might possibly be in the air. Heaven help him if she spotted him, outside the clairvoyante's bungalow. He would get no peace until she found out what was going on. In any event, she was going to find out that he had been over to the village that afternoon. The Dixons would see to that. They were in their garden and had waved to him as he had driven past.

He thought about the Dixons for a moment, wondered if they would know where the clairvoyante might be. He made a small bet with himself that they would. They looked as though they had been working out-of-doors for hours.

He left his car and walked back along the road towards the Dixons' comparatively new bungalow, thinking about his aunt, what he would tell her when she telephoned to-night. . . .

The Dixons, who were still digging in their garden, were not aware of David Sayer's presence until he spoke. Their back lawn, with which they were principally occupied, was a mess, pockmarked with scores of tiny holes. And the source of the peculiar smell which filled the air and which David had at first been unable to identify—because one hardly expected the Dixons, even though they were known to be neurotic about their billiards table–smooth lawn, to *moth-*

proof it—came indeed from mothballs, the hundreds the Dixons were now feverishly burying in the holes they had spent all day digging.

"To rid us of the moles, of course," Philip Dixon explained in response to David's bemused inquiry. "We've tried everything else, spent a fortune on baits. And there aren't all that many mole catchers around these days. Mothballs are our last resort. The perishers have undermined the garden shed —see the lean it's got"—David looked and was genuinely amazed at the outbuilding's drunken list—"but it's the bungalow we're worried about. That could be their next target, the experts tell us."

"It works, does it?" inquired David. "Mothballs?"

"Cyril Forbes said it does," replied Philip Dixon.

"Oh, yes," said David. "Cyril Forbes." (Enough said, he thought.)

"Mrs. Charles went over to Gidding again today. He didn't go, though . . . her brother. She was on her own this time."

It was Mrs. Dixon who volunteered this information, in between carefully counting mothballs into one of the holes in the lawn.

"We saw her on the special Gidding market bus when it went past, didn't we, Philip? She must've done some shopping in the village first and then caught the bus down there instead of picking it up at the bottom of the road like she usually does."

Philip Dixon agreed, then moved on a couple of paces and started on another hole. David drifted away during the long discussion which then ensued between the Dixons as to the exact number of holes that should be dug in the lawn and whether there would be enough mothballs to fill them all. It was some fifteen minutes later that Mr. Dixon noted that David was nowhere to be seen and that his car—when Mr. Dixon walked out to the road to check—had also disappeared and was now no longer standing outside the clairvoyante's bungalow. "I wonder what Sayer wanted with Edwina Charles?" he remarked on his return.

His wife said, "Maybe it was something to do with that prowler, the man they're saying down in the village used to be one of her old boyfriends. Didn't Mr. Sayer call on her the other day about him?"

"That's what Stan North said. But Sayer also called on us about him, so that doesn't mean anything. Not unless the fellow's one of your old flames too, my precious."

They lapsed into silence. Then, straightening up, Mrs. Dixon said, "Do you really think this will work, Philip?"

The address Enid Flegg had given Mrs. Charles was on the south side of Gidding, a short five-minute bus ride from the town centre.

Twelve Enterprise Walk was a large, semidetached, double-fronted house with only a narrow strip of begonia-planted front garden no more than three feet in width. Thus it was that Mrs. Charles, on arriving at this address soon after lunch on the day following her visit to Mrs. Flegg, was able to stand on the footpath outside the low brick fence and read the typewritten postcard which was discreetly displayed in the lower left-hand front window.

MME. M. LAFFONT

FRENCH LESSONS

ADVANCED OR BEGINNERS

FULLY-TRAINED PROFESSIONAL TEACHER.

Mme. Laffont ("Mrs., actually," she confided to the clairvoyante when the latter had explained the purpose of her visit) looked in her late fifties but was probably a lot older. She wore a calf-length black skirt with an orchid pink, lacy jumper over a massive forty-four–inch bosom. Around her neck, perhaps in an endeavour to conceal the advanced years she feared the fragile skin of her throat might betray, was a wide, pearl-beaded neckband. Long pearl earrings dangled from bloodless, pendulous earlobes. Her hair, which was tinted a harsh shade of auburn, was waved in the style of the twenties and cut very short at the back like a man's. An excessive application of moisturising lotion highlighted the fine lines around her eyes, but this, and a little carefully applied mascara, was all the makeup she wore on what would once have been a flawless English rose complexion.

The small sitting room into which Mrs. Charles was ushered reflected an exquisite taste in antique furniture that would have been totally unexpected had the clairvoyante not first met Alice.

If Mimi Laffont was the teacher, then Alice (no last name was volunteered)—Mimi's older sister—was surely the head-mistress.

Alice was wearing a tailored grey linen dress, pinned to the left shoulder of which was an exquisitely delicate platinum brooch fashioned in the shape of a leaf. A pair of pince-nez hung on a long silver chain around her neck. Her grey hair was cut, like her sister's, in a severely short but not unflattering style, and she too wore little, if any, makeup at all. While Mimi would almost certainly have once been very pretty, Alice had been, and still was, a striking-looking woman.

Alice did most of the talking in a cultured, beautifully modulated voice which was remarkably similar in tone and pitch to her sister's.

Tony Manners and her invalid father, she explained to the clairvoyante, became tenants of their furnished upstairs flat somewhere around four years ago. Alice confirmed that Mr. Manners was a gravely ill man who was, for the greater part of the Manners's tenancy, confined to his bed; also that it was as Mrs. Flegg had said, Mimi used to pop upstairs every so often during the day to make sure he was all right and that there was nothing he needed.

"Tony had no one else who could call round during the day and lend a hand with Mr. Manners," Alice went on. "At least, that was what she gave us to understand. Isn't that right, Mimi?"

Alice glanced into the gloomiest corner of the room, where Mimi always took herself when the sisters had guests and the daylight was inclined to be harsh and revealing.

Mimi said, "Tony didn't really talk about herself, though, did she, Alice? We might rather have assumed that she had no family, mightn't we?"

"Did either of you ever meet any of her friends?" inquired Mrs. Charles.

Out of the gloom came a solemn no from Mimi, while Alice said, "No one ever came here—to the flat—to see either of them. Can you ever remember anyone coming?" she asked her sister.

Mimi said, "Because of him, we always thought, didn't we, Alice? People shy away when they know there's sickness about the place. They don't want to get involved. People simply don't have the time to be neighbourly like in the old days."

"You've relet the flat, I suppose?"

The abruptness of the clairvoyante's question took the sisters by surprise, and they looked at one another quickly. Mimi was the first to recover. She opened her mouth to say something but was silenced by Alice's sharp, "Yes. Two young French girls—students—who are over here to improve their English, moved in several weeks ago."

"Can you tell me then what happened to Tony's things— the contents of the flat?" The clairvoyante, looking from Alice to Mimi, raised her eyebrows and added, "Seeing as there was no next of kin that anyone seems to know about."

This time Alice wasn't quite quick enough.

"Mr. Hammond . . ." said Mimi. "The man who owns the building in town where Tony rented an office? He took away most of her things—the typewriter and what little furniture Tony and her father had brought with them. He said it was his. In a manner of speaking, that is."

Alice said smoothly (and somehow defensively, the clairvoyante thought), "Mr. Hammond was perfectly within his rights, of course. Tony was behind with her rent. I understand he was owed a considerable sum of money. And as we've said, there was no family to consider."

"You said there was a typewriter?" Mrs. Charles looked at Mimi. "Tony brought work home from the office?"

Mimi hesitated and Alice stepped in smartly and said, "We wouldn't really know about that. Once Tony came home we rarely went near the flat."

"Were either of you present when Mr. Hammond removed the things from the flat?"

"Of course," said Alice. Her voice was noticeably cooler, as if the question had affronted her and she wished to make that fact plain. "And again later when the police came and took away her papers."

"They were trying to trace her family," Mimi chipped in. "They thought there might be some mention of someone— in a will, perhaps—but they didn't find anything, did they, Alice? Tony was quite alone in the world. Except for us."

"Would you happen to know where Tony and her father lived before moving into your flat?"

"Lymstead, we believe," said Alice, looking steadily at her sister. After a moment, her face relaxed into a grave yet faintly challenging smile. "But we don't know whereabouts in Lymstead, do we, Mimi?"

Mimi appeared to be shaking her head (the clairvoyante wasn't sure whether in agreement with or in reproof of her sister's reply).

"They never said, and we never asked," Alice added for good measure.

Mrs. Charles looked at her for a moment. Then she said, "Forgive my impertinence, but I understand you own a dog —a poodle?—and that Tony used to walk him for you."

Alice's eyes widened a little. "Yes," she said. "That is correct. Pierre."

"He's at the beauty parlour this afternoon," Mimi piped up. "Tony was very fond of him. He still looks for her. If he thinks we're not watching, he sneaks upstairs and scratches at the door for her to take him out for his early evening walkies."

"Did Tony ever mention an incident which took place between her and the owner of the pet shop in town—the Birdarama—when she was out one time with your dog?"

"Mr. Krendel, you mean?" asked Mimi.

"No," said Alice in reply to Mrs. Charles's question. She shook her head at her sister. "We weren't aware that she walked Pierre that far, were we, Mimi?" She laughed. "No wonder he came home some evenings all fagged out and did nothing but sleep."

Mrs. Charles, rising to leave, paused and looked at the sisters thoughtfully. They were either covering something up or they were worried about something. In either case, though, it might not necessarily be anything directly concerned with her inquiries on behalf of the mysterious Mr. Valentine, as she was increasingly finding herself thinking of him. At this stage, she would be more inclined to think that the defensive tone of voice which Alice had used when speaking of Mr. Hammond pointed at their knowing one another on an intimate basis, and that was why Mr. Hammond had been permitted access to their tenant's flat and its contents ahead of anyone else. An action which Alice might since have regretted condoning (or suspected might have serious repercussions for them and was therefore on guard against).

Both sisters accompanied Mrs. Charles to the door. Mimi stepped back into the protective shadow of the hallstand as the door opened to avoid any daylight falling directly on her face. Mrs. Charles, looking past Alice to say good-bye, tried to see into her eyes, but Alice, as if reading her thoughts, moved deliberately between them.

Stepping out onto the porch, Mrs. Charles was suddenly confronted by the tall, uniformed police officer who had been about to step up and ring the bell as the door had opened.

She looked at him, startled by his unexpected appearance,

murmured "good afternoon," then looked back at Alice with a mildly questioning glance and politely excused herself.

As she walked the few steps to the gate she heard the policeman say, "Afternoon ladies . . . Being good girls, are we?"

When she turned to shut the gate, the sisters and the policeman had disappeared behind the closed front door.

The day, while clear-skied and sunny, was much cooler than the previous one and so Mrs. Charles decided to walk back into the town centre. Out of the corner of an eye, she saw the net curtains on the living room window of the house directly across the road twitch slightly, and two doors further down a woman suddenly appeared in an upstairs window and pretended to make some fussy adjustments to the folds of her nets.

Both sets of eyes thoughtfully monitored Mrs. Charles's progress down the street.

CHAPTER SIX

Mrs. Charles had covered half the length of Enterprise Walk when she heard the short, pattering footsteps coming up swiftly behind her. Looking round, she saw a stout woman in a lumpy grey coat. A floppy, wide-brimmed grey felt hat obscured the woman's head and face. In her right hand was a white leather dog leash clipped to a matching red and blue rhinestone-studded leather collar. The woman, who walked with her eyes lowered, didn't see Mrs. Charles and pulled up sharply, jerking back her head with a startled "Oh!" when she reached her.

It was Mimi Laffont.

She glanced uneasily across the road, where an elderly white-haired woman, having drawn aside the net curtain on her front window, stared openly at her.

Mimi made some delicate fluttering movements with her arms and hands which reminded the clairvoyante of the fragile butterfly she had once watched defensively warding off the probings of a puppy's inquisitive snout. Then, turning her back on the woman in the window and lowering her head and her voice, Mimi said, "I was hoping I'd catch up with you, Mrs. Charles. I wanted to ask you something about Tony."

With her head still lowered Mimi glanced furtively back along the street towards her home as if she expected, or feared, that someone there might be taking the same kind of interest in her as was the woman watching from the other side of the road.

"I've got to go into the town centre to fetch Pierre. He

should be done by now. I thought that if you were going that way too, we might walk together."

Mimi raised her head a little and made a mild grimace. "I hate having to go and fetch him, it's not fair. It's always me who has to go out and get him. The girl at the beauty parlour collects him, but she won't deliver him back home after his clip and shampoo. Tony always used to do that for us, bring him home with her when she'd finished work for the day. I really do miss her for that," she finished with a wistful sigh.

They started along the footpath, Mimi with her head lowered and the brim of her hat flapping about her face like elephant ears.

"What was it you wanted to ask me about Tony?" inquired Mrs. Charles.

Mimi hesitated. Then in a doubtful voice, she asked, "You don't really suspect foul play, do you?"

"No," admitted the clairvoyante. "However, as I explained to you and your sister, my client does, and he's going to be a very difficult man to persuade to change his mind."

"Is he some sort of relative of Tony's?" asked Mimi hesitatingly and with a quick nervous glance behind them.

"I don't honestly know. He never said."

"Oh," said Mimi. She was quiet for a minute. Then, "Alice will be furious with me if she finds out I've told you this, but I don't care, I think I should . . . you know, just in case. And it was odd—even Alice said it was odd—the way Tony asked us to promise that we'd destroy her files if anything should ever happen to her."

Mimi hesitated. Then, with a quick glance at her companion, "You remember what you said about the Birdarama—that Mr. Krendel? Well, there was something about him in the papers we burnt. I didn't mean to look, but the file was so bulky—mainly because of the newspaper Tony had stuffed into it—that when I went to throw it into the incinerator to burn, some loose sheets of paper slipped out. One of the sheets I picked up and glanced at had Mr. Krendel's name on it (and some dates, I think) and a list of what might have been the proper names—the breed, I mean—of some birds. Finch and suchlike."

Mrs. Charles paused on the footpath and stared at her. "What files were these, Mrs. Laffont? The ones in Tony's office?"

Mimi, likewise pausing, shook her head. "Tony must've had two sets of files—the ones the police took from her office and the ones we found upstairs. We don't really know. . . . That's just what we decided when we were talking about it afterwards with Mr. Hammond."

"You destroyed everything?"

The elephant ears flapped up and down as Mimi nodded. "Naturally we didn't touch any of Tony's personal papers. She never said anything about them so we left them for the police to find. We just emptied out the small safe. There wasn't much in it," she concluded on an apologetic note. "Just the one big file and a few loose papers."

"Did you look at any of the loose papers?"

"No. We were in rather a hurry, actually. Mr. Hammond phoned to tell us what had happened to Tony (he'd been tipped the wink by someone he knows at the police station) —I think he really wanted to know if the police had been round to see us. Anyway, Alice said they hadn't and he said he'd be straight round."

Mimi's lips came together disapprovingly. "I don't know what Alice sees in that man. She's *besotted* with him. *Mean!* You wouldn't believe the lengths that man would go to to save a miserable halfpenny. And that office of Tony's . . . I don't know how the poor girl stood it. All those fumes coming up from the dry cleaner's. It's his shop, you know. The couple who run it are only employees. And those headaches Tony used to get . . . It's no wonder she finished up depressed and suicidal."

"Did Mr. Hammond have any part in the burning of Tony's papers—the ones you took from the flat?"

"He did not. I saw to that!" Mimi tossed her head, and the elephant ears flew out indignantly. "They were out of that flat and down on the fire long before he showed up. The old skinflint finished up with her newspaper, though. We don't take the *Sketch*, and Alice wanted to read it. We don't take any papers, actually. Alice won't go down to the newsagent and pay for them to be delivered, and I don't see why I should always be the one who has to go out and do all the fetching and carrying. Alice knows how I hate to feel the sun on my skin. It makes me feel all shrivelled up like a dried apricot."

"The newspaper was a recent one, was it?"

"That day's. That is, the day she died, Friday the tenth of June."

"Had anything been removed from it?" asked Mrs. Charles. Then, in response to the inquiring look Mimi gave her, "I don't suppose you noticed if something had been cut or torn out of it or whether anything had been ringed or marked in any way?"

"Not that I can remember," said Mimi with a slow shake of her head. "I only managed a quick glance at it before Alice called out to me that Shylock—Mr. Hammond—had turned up. And then, as I've said, the old skinflint pocketed it. Do you know that man has the nerve to go into a butcher's shop and buy one sausage for his dinner? *One measly sausage.* The thin type too!"

"Did Mr. Hammond know about this file of Tony's?"

"Yes, Alice told him as soon as he arrived what we'd done." Mimi's head came up, and she eyed Mrs. Charles scornfully. "She tells him everything."

"Did he seem at all bothered about it?"

"Only for her, Alice, I think. He said we really ought to have handed everything over to the police. But a promise is a promise. And why should we do the police any favours? They've never done us any."

"When did Tony ask you to destroy the papers she showed you?"

"The day she died. That afternoon. She came home early and said she was making a trip to Glasgow that night on an unexpected business matter. And then she told us what we were to do with the papers in her safe if anything happened to her. It seemed a bit strange at the time, but then we never thought any more of it after it all came out at the inquest about how depressed and worried she'd been. We already knew about the terrible heads she'd been getting—they were one of the reasons why she liked to get out for a breath of fresh air with Pierre."

"Did Tony say anything to you about her visit that day to Mr. Bing?"

"The spiritual healer?" Mimi shook her head. "No, she never talked much about personal things."

Slowly they continued walking down the street. After a minute or two, Mimi said, "Most people would think this is a very strange thing to say—particularly as I used to look in on Mr. Manners most days—but I learned more about Tony and her father from Tony's inquest than I ever did through talking to either one of them. Mr. Manners had even less to say than she did. He was a very polite, well-educated man, but terribly reserved—the kind who, when you try to start up a conversation, will end it with a one sentence reply. Like the time I remarked how lucky he was to have Tony for a daughter, and he said that his good fortune was her misfortune and that she was a victim and would always be a victim, just like he was. Well, I ask you . . . What can a person say to that?"

Mimi was momentarily silent. Then, "I don't know why, but I've never forgotten it—the way he spoke about Tony that day. Even now it makes me feel sad. It was as though he knew Tony was doomed, and yet he still clung to her like grim death, draining the life out of her, when he really should've insisted that he went into hospital or a nursing home. Tony had had one nervous breakdown. He must've known that the chances were that put under too much pressure she'd have another. And her first breakdown must've been quite a serious one for her to have been sent to The Grange. Rosa Trumble only takes hopeless cases—the ones everybody else has given up on."

There was something about the way Mimi spoke which suggested that she was speaking not from hearsay but from personal experience—either her own or that of someone quite close to her.

"This came out at the inquest?" inquired Mrs. Charles.

Mimi shook her head. "No, no mention was made of either Mrs. Trumble or The Grange at the inquest. Mr. Hammond had his wife, Julia, committed there—to The Grange—when he found out she'd been writing cheques all over town without his consent for a whole load of stuff neither of them wanted. Knowing that old skinflint, I was convinced she'd never come out of the place. I couldn't see him taking that kind of risk again, not with his most prized possession, his beloved cheque-book. I thought that when the time came for her to be sent home, he'd find some excuse for having her kept there. But I was wrong about that. Julia eventually recovered and went home—no doubt, like Tony, thanks to Rosa Trumble. She's a most remarkable woman. Alice and I met her once when Mr. Hammond persuaded us to go along with him to a spiritualists' meeting over in Lymstead soon after Julia died. Mrs. Trumble practises this holistic medicine that one hears so much about today. Actually she's like that Mr. Bing. She's a spiritual healer."

Mrs. Charles looked at Mimi thoughtfully. "I wonder why Tony didn't go and see her instead of Mr. Bing?"

"Yes, we wondered about that," admitted Mimi. "Perhaps she got in touch with Mrs. Trumble and she recommended Mr. Bing."

"If the nursing home where Tony had her breakdown wasn't referred to by name at the inquest, how do you know which one it was? Did Tony tell you?"

"No. A letter came for her once readdressed from The Grange, and the postman pushed it through our letter slot by mistake. Of course we knew straightaway what it meant. And in some ways, we weren't terribly surprised. Tony wasn't a weak person, you understand, but we both felt there was something fragile about her. She tended to be too quiet and withdrawn. And it didn't seem natural for her to be so much on her own, with no friends."

Mrs. Charles nodded. "Whereabouts is this nursing home?"

"It's in Lymstead. I don't know about now—it was some years ago that we met her—but at that time, Mrs. Trumble was one of the leading lights in the spiritualist movement there."

They had paused to cross the road, and Mimi, looking to the right down Enterprise Walk, suddenly bobbed her head and said, "Don't look—" Her eyes beneath her floppy hat brim sparkled mischievously. She looked years younger. "It's Old Bill."

A white police car slowed as it reached the two women waiting at the kerb, and the driver—the constable who had called at 12 Enterprise Walk a short while earlier—ducked his head to look at them.

He was not so much interested in Mimi Laffont as in the tall, elegant blonde with her.

"Mrs. Edwina Charles, eh?" he murmured to himself. He had heard that name somewhere before. . . . In connection with the Laffont sisters? A bit upmarket for those two old tarts, wasn't she? Still, Alice, in her heyday, had been pretty upmarket, mixed only with the nobs. Or so they said. . . .

CHAPTER SEVEN

Mrs. Charles sat at a small table in the cramped Dickensian reading room of the Gidding *Daily Sketch*. She had been sitting there for over half an hour carefully going through the June tenth edition—the day on which Tony Manners had visited Benjamin Bing, the faith healer, and then later taken a train north to Scotland.

There were two items which Mrs. Charles considered might have been of interest to the young private inquiry agent on that particular day. The second item was a brief report near the back of the paper concerning the progress a consortium of bird fanciers (headed by a Mrs. Dolly Dackers of Lymstead) was making in the search for the organised crime ring which was allegedly stealing valuable birds, not only from local breeders but also from the owners of several large private estates in the county which kept aviaries of exotic rare birds.

This, in the clairvoyante's opinion, seemed the most logical reason for the newspaper to have been stuffed inside the file Mimi Laffont claimed had contained at least one reference to Neville Krendel, the proprietor of the Birdarama. It followed then that there was a distinct possibility that Tony had indeed been keeping both Krendel and his pet shop under surveillance in connection with a genuine birdnapping, as Jimmy Valentine had termed it. It could be mere coincidence that there had been some past bitterness between Mrs. Dackers and Krendel over his having jilted Mrs. Dackers for her daughter, but Mrs. Charles instinctively doubted it. Human nature being what it was, in some way— even if only tenuously—the two would be linked.

According to the newspaper report, the police (to quote Mrs. Dackers, who had obviously been in a tetchy frame of mind at the time) ". . . were useless, getting nowhere fast." And hence the need, Mrs. Charles supposed, for the bird fanciers consortium to hire the services of a private inquiry agent.

It all fitted nicely. Too nicely? she wondered with a frown. But surely (this was supposing that Jimmy Valentine was right and that Tony Manners was murdered) private inquiry agents—a mere girl in this instance—didn't get pushed to their deaths from speeding Glasgow-bound express trains because they were hot on the trail of a gang of bird thieves. Drug traffickers, maybe, where millions of pounds could be at stake. Or something somebody might hold as dear as money, mused Mrs. Charles. There couldn't possibly be all that much at stake over a few rare birds. It was an area, though, of which she had no knowledge, and so she was reluctant to dismiss it entirely as being unlikely. For all she knew, a rare breeding bird might be worth as much as some racehorses became after their racing life was over and they were put out to stud.

She decided to keep an open mind on the matter until she had made a few inquiries from some suitably informed source.

The other item she had come across was much more puzzling. Puzzling because on the surface it would seem that it could have been as a result of reading this particular news item that Tony had gone dashing out of the Half Moon that morning to see Benjamin Bing—without even waiting to finish her tea. Tony had been reading the paper (presumably the *Sketch)* when Jimmy Valentine walked in: then, according to Jill, Tony had quickly got up and left (to avoid the unwelcome attentions of Jimmy Valentine, the young waitress had been encouraged to suppose by her more worldly employer, Mrs. Wong). Always a possibility, of course, thought Mrs. Charles; but not if what Jimmy Valentine had said were true. He claimed that Tony had told him she was going to see a man about a ghost. And that man had more than likely been Benjamin Bing.

But only if the ghost Tony had referred to that morning was that of her father.

Frowning, Mrs. Charles looked again at the front page of the *Sketch* for June tenth.

The headlines for that day were black and heavy.

HANGING JUDGE DIES IN BIZARRE ACCIDENT

Late last evening, the newspaper report ran, *Mr. Justice Halahan—once known as "the hanging judge" and best remembered for the sensational Pym murder trial eleven years ago—died after accidentally hanging himself in his bedroom at his country mansion situated on the outskirts of Lymstead.*

Mr. John Ramsay, Mr. Justice Halahan's butler, found his employer hanging by a rope from a wooden curtain rail in his bedroom when he returned from a spiritualists' meeting in Lymstead soon after 11 P.M. Mr. Justice Halahan died moments later in his butler's arms, his last words to him being, "Tell Bing. Pain back." Mr. Ramsay explained that this cryptic message undoubtedly referred to the severe migraine headaches which Mr. Justice Halahan had been suffering and which Mr. Bing, a noted spiritual healer, had been treating, and with considerable success, Mr. Ramsay reported. Mr. Justice Halahan had not complained of head pain for some weeks.

An additional bizarre feature of the judge's death was the way his right hand was taped to the side of his head over his right ear with wide strips of sticking plaster. When questioned by the police about this, Mr. Ramsay could offer no explanation other than to surmise that his employer—a lifelong eccentric—had taped his hand in this position possibly as part of the head and neck exercises a chiropractor had once recommended to him, which included a form of "hanging" by the neck. Normally this latter "exercise," Mr. Ram-

say explained, was only ever done under the strict supervision of the chiropractor at his consulting rooms.

A spokesman for the police said that foul play was not suspected and that it seemed more than likely that Mr. Justice Halahan, while suffering an acute migraine attack, had foolishly attempted to alleviate his pain by hanging himself as prescribed by his chiropractor, but unfortunately with fatal results.

The newspaper report then went on to say that due to the timely intervention of Mr. Ramsay, who cut the judge down from the rope attached to the curtain rail, the judge's death was not as a result of hanging but from delayed shock.

There followed a short but stern warning from a prominent local chiropractor pointing out the obvious dangers in anyone attempting anything similar without proper medical supervision.

The report concluded with a brief resume of the judge's career, which had culminated with the sensational murder trial of the well-known stage and television actor of the time, Rendell Maxwell Pym.

Mrs. Charles closed the newspaper file and leaned back in her chair, then closed her eyes.

Mr. Justice Halahan's migraines, the headaches Mimi Laffont (and others) claimed Tony used to suffer—this too, in its own way, fitted, explained why Tony might have felt the sudden urge to see Benjamin Bing.

But then in that case, how did one arrive at the statement she had made to Jimmy Valentine about a ghost?

Didn't it all amount to the same thing? Tony's headaches, her depression, could so easily have led to her brooding morbidly and obsessively about her health, which, almost certainly, would have conjured up the terrible visions of the hereditary illness she feared.

But why go to see Benjamin Bing so suddenly? Why hadn't she gone back to Rosa Trumble, the spiritualist who had helped her once before?

This, thought Mrs. Charles, was the question to be answered. If she could get a satisfactory explanation there, then she would take Cyril's advice and summon Jimmy Valentine to convince him that his young lady friend had taken her own life.

Mrs. Charles looked at the time. It was a few minutes to three. She could be in Lymstead by four. . . .

She considered for a moment. Yes, the direct approach would be best. She would get far more from Rosa Trumble in a face-to-face meeting than by attempting to get any answers over the telephone.

And there was another reason for preferring not to speak by telephone with Rosa Trumble: the element of surprise. A useful weapon to have when at the back of the clairvoyante's mind was a nagging awareness that no matter now which way she turned, she found herself walking in a circle around the one central theme.

The Lymstead Spiritualists' Society.

Mrs. Charles sat at the rear of the bus reading the copy of the *Sketch* she had bought on leaving the newspaper offices. She had turned to the public notices at the back. The combined Gidding and Lymstead Spiritualists' societies were holding a meeting in the church hall in Gidding next Tuesday night, she noted. Guest speaker, on this occasion, was to be Mr. John Ramsay, who would give a talk on "The Modern Medium." Visitors, she also noted, were welcome.

She looked up quickly when a bright familiar voice said, "It's Mrs. Charles, isn't it?"

The clairvoyante smiled. It was Enid Flegg.

Mrs. Charles made room on the seat beside her for the other woman to sit down. Mrs. Flegg looked in a cheery frame of mind, which seemed a hopeful sign that the robbery and escape to London which her son had planned for the previous night had not materialised. His girlfriend, as the clairvoyante had suspected, was some way off still from being talked into becoming his accomplice.

Mrs. Flegg sat down with a small sigh. "Ah, that's better. My feet are killing me!" She smiled quickly. "Are you going into Lymstead?"

Mrs. Charles said she was.

"It's a lovely little place—much nicer, I think, than Gidding," said Mrs. Flegg. "My son and I lived over there until the man I used to housekeep for, Dr. MacDonald, retired. He went back home to Scotland, which left us with nowhere to live—it was a live-in position. Mr. Hammond handled the sale of Dr. MacDonald's house, and he suggested that my boy, Trev, and I should move over here, where there was more work. Dr. MacDonald wanted me to go with him, but Trev wasn't keen—all his friends are here—and then there's my sister Liz. She still lives over in Lymstead, and I didn't really want to be too far from her. She doesn't have the best of health—I'm on my way to see her now, as a matter of fact. She left a phone message with my neighbour that she's had another of her queer giddy turns. Psychosomatic, Dr. Mac-Donald said they were. But giving them a fancy name doesn't cure them, does it?"

"Anyway," she went on, "as it happened, it all turned out for the best as far as Trev and I were concerned. Dr. Mac-Donald died not long after he went back to Scotland, so I would've been out on a limb anyhow. It was a terrible business. I was upset about it for days. Dr. MacDonald was robbed and beaten up, murdered—in a church graveyard, of all places. He used to go and sit there every afternoon and compose church music, and then when he'd got it all in his head, he'd slip inside the church and play it on the organ and get it down on paper."

Tears suddenly came into Mrs. Flegg's eyes, and she quickly blinked them away.

"The sadistic beasts who killed him put tape over his eyes so he couldn't identify them."

Mrs. Charles stared at her, and Mrs. Flegg nodded. "Yes, you heard right. . . . Sticking plaster! They put his hands over his eyes, then taped them there with long strips of sticking plaster. Then they beat him up and robbed him and left him to die. A tourist found him, some elderly American who was in the graveyard looking at the old tombstones, trying to trace his ancestors. He'll have taken home a wonderful impression of the British people, I must say!"

"When did this happen, Mrs. Flegg?"

The expression on the clairvoyante's face puzzled Mrs. Flegg. She replied slowly. "About four or five months ago. Why?"

The bemused look in the clairvoyante's eye gave way to a steady frown.

"Did you discuss any of this with Tony Manners?"

"Well, yes . . . of course—I couldn't help myself. I was so upset when I heard from my sister what had happened that I cried for days afterwards. Dr. MacDonald was such a kind, gentle man."

"Can you think back, Mrs. Flegg? This could be very important. Did Tony make any comment when you told her what had happened to the doctor?"

Mrs. Flegg frowned. "Not that I can remember. She just listened, same as always. I talk rather a lot, you know," she pointed out with a rueful smile. "Liz, my sister, is forever complaining that she can't get a word in edgewise with me, and that when she finally does I don't always hear what she's said. I'm too busy thinking about what I'm going to say next, she says."

"Did Tony appear to be upset by what you'd told her?"

Mrs. Flegg shook her head. "No—why should she be? It wasn't as though she knew Dr. MacDonald."

"Are you quite sure about that?"

Mrs. Flegg stared at her.

"Couldn't Tony have been one of the doctor's patients at some time or another? Her father, perhaps? Couldn't he have been one of his patients?"

"I suppose so. . . . I don't really know. That never occurred to me." Mrs. Flegg hesitated, frowned. "Tony never lived in Lymstead, did she?"

"Yes. She was once a patient in a nursing home there. The Grange, I believe it was called, run by a Mrs. Rosa Trumble."

"Oh yes, *her*," said Mrs. Flegg in a dry voice. Her eyes widened. "I do hope you're not going over to Lymstead thinking you're going to call round at The Grange about Tony. You're a bit late if you are. The place was closed down ages ago by the local authority, who objected to Mrs. Trumble's unorthodox methods. They kept warning her they'd close her down, but she took no notice. She's in Australia now, I believe. I think my sister told me Mrs. Trumble has a married daughter out there, and she's gone to live with her."

Mrs. Flegg paused. Then, "Are you absolutely sure Tony was one of Rosa Trumble's patients?"

"Quite sure."

Mrs. Flegg shook her head and made a series of soft clicking noises with her tongue. "That just goes to show you, doesn't it? You never know. . . ."

"What don't you know, Mrs. Flegg?" asked Mrs. Charles when the other woman paused.

"Well, Tony—" Mrs. Flegg looked distinctly embarrassed. "The Grange was a mental home, you know. Mrs. Trumble's patients were mostly psychopaths, schizo-whatever they call it when you think you're two people. That's what Dr. MacDonald said, anyway. The husband of one of his patients finished up there. It was a long while ago, but you might have heard of him. Rendell Pym? He used to be on the television all the time, quite a big celebrity." Mrs. Flegg's eyes widened slowly. "Surely you remember him—'the man everybody loved to hate?' The one who murdered his wife."

CHAPTER EIGHT

Mrs. Charles stepped down from the bus, waved at Mrs. Flegg's smiling face, which was pressed close to the window, and nodded when Mrs. Flegg pointed to the street immediately on the clairvoyante's left.

It was in this street that Rosa Trumble's nursing home had once been located.

Following Mrs. Flegg's directions, Mrs. Charles found herself outside a large, red brick Victorian house set back a short distance from the road and standing on a sweeping semicircular drive. A black, gold-lettered board to the right of the tall wrought-iron gates identified the property as being the Brayside Infants School.

An elderly man was poking about with a white-tipped walking stick in one of the flower beds bordering the drive near the gates. His back was to Mrs. Charles. She watched him for a minute or two, then, raising her voice a little, she said, "Excuse me. I'm sorry to trouble you, but I wonder if you could help me, please?"

The old man stopped poking in the flower bed, looked round, then walked slowly over to her.

They conducted their conversation through the iron bars of the double gates, which were closed and padlocked for the summer holidays.

"Would this be The Grange?" she inquired.

"As was," replied the old man. He raised his stick at the signboard. "Council, in its infinite wisdom, saw fit to close the place down. Infants school now. Proper little bunch of anarchists! Mustn't upset the little dears. . . . If Master Tommy feels like eating grass today," he said in a forced, falsetto voice, "then we mustn't go running about the playground brandishing our walking stick and bellowing at him, must we, Mr. Fullbright?" His voice took on a low growl. "Never mind that not ten minutes since, nasty Mr. Fullbright sprayed all the perishing grass with weed killer and that Master Tommy is now going to need a stomach pump!"

And grumbling to himself, the old man ambled off towards the school building, pausing every now and again to poke his stick at something he had spotted in the flower beds, and then finally stepping carefully through the beds to the lawn beyond when he suddenly spied a solitary plantain. He stood over it and scowled. A good pinch of sulphate of ammonia dead in its heart would soon see that off.

Nodding, he turned and headed for the outbuildings to the rear of the main building where the gardener's needs were kept. . . .

Now that was an odd coincidence, he thought as he shuffled along: two people turning up like this on the one day—within an hour of one another too—and going on about The Grange.

A black Labrador dog with arthritis in both hind legs waddled stiffly into view and half cocked a leg over a red geranium. The old man let out a roar and charged towards him with his stick raised.

Ellen Purdie was saying, "But they'll have to put Trigger down, Dad. The Council will make them. They can't keep him. Please, Dad. Just for a few days while they keep looking for a home for him."

"No," said Purdie. "They knew there was a Council ban on pets before they bought the dog, didn't they?"

"Well yes," the girl admitted. "But it would've been all right if it hadn't been for the mean old cow who lives next door. Even the man from the Council said it would've been all right if she hadn't complained."

Purdie said nothing.

"Please, Dad. I'll make sure he keeps right out of your way. You won't even know he's here."

Purdie looked pointedly at the clock on the wall above the row of spirits dispensers. "It's time you were opening up. They'll be breaking down the door in a minute."

She looked at him angrily. Miserable old pig. That was all he cared about, his rotten pub! Well, she'd show him; she'd do what Trev wanted and then they'd run away to London together. And she'd take Trigger with her!

Out of the corner of his eye, Purdie watched his daughter flounce across the public bar to unlock the door to the street. Subconsciously he fingered a small scar under his right eye. He felt upset, not about his argument with Ellen, but the way he always did when the talk was of dogs, which aroused too many unpleasant memories. He had felt uneasy all afternoon, ever since his trip to The Grange, he reflected. That old boy's vile dog had *actually growled at him,* and for no reason at all! They knew, didn't they?—sensed it when you didn't like them.

Purdie shuddered and made himself think of something else. After a few minutes, his coarse, hirsute features relaxed into a small smile. Fullbright hadn't taken him seriously. No one would. That was the beauty of it.

Purdie ignored the malevolent look his daughter flung at him and stepped aside as she flounced back to the bar counter. He smiled to himself as he picked up his train of thought and carried on with it. Yes, that was the whole secret. . . . No one would ever suspect. *Not even the next victim.*

Purdie's eyes narrowed. Well, nobody could say that the bad-tempered old devil hadn't been given fair warning.

Purdie tried to muster some enjoyment out of his situation, but his uneasiness increased. He was beginning to regret having gone over to The Grange: he wasn't even sure now why he had bothered. Frowning, he wondered if it had something to do with the girl. It had been wrong to kill her: he'd thought so all along.

Purdie nodded to himself. Yes, that was why he'd felt he ought to give Fullbright a sporting chance at least. To make up for her . . .

Mrs. Charles found David Sayer's business card lying on the carpet near the front door when she got home that evening. On the back of it he had sketched a large eye, and beside it was an exclamation mark. Mrs. Charles wasn't sure whether the exclamation mark expressed his exasperation at finding her out when he had called again or whether he had some information for her concerning Tony Manners.

The telephone rang while she was looking at the card. It was Jimmy Valentine, wanting to know how her inquiries were progressing.

"Slowly," she responded.

"When do you think you'll have something for me?" he asked when she made no further comment.

"I'm not sure, Mr. Valentine. I've yet to be convinced that there's anything there for you."

"Oh, there's something there, all right," he said after a slight pause. "You'd have been back to me sooner if there wasn't. I'll be over your way on some other business on Tuesday night. I'll call in and we'll have a little chat."

"No, Tuesday won't be convenient, Mr. Valentine. I won't be in. I'm going to see a man about a ghost."

There was a long pause. Then Jimmy Valentine said, "The last person who said that to me finished up dead not a day later." There was another pause. Then he went on, "I take it you're planning on seeing Bing."

"Not him necessarily. But if he happens to be about I'll probably have a word with him."

There was a long silence. Then Jimmy Valentine said, "Don't go taking no train trips afterwards, will you?"

"No, Mr. Valentine. I promise you I won't do that."

David Sayer called to see the clairvoyante the following morning at eleven as arranged between them when she telephoned him after talking to Jimmy Valentine.

Mrs. Charles poured coffee from the steaming percolator, which had been standing on one side awaiting his arrival. Then, sitting down, she smiled and said, "Now to business. You've got something interesting for me, you said?"

"Nothing much. But it might prove useful. That's if you're pressing on with your inquiries into the girl's death?" He paused expectantly, but Mrs. Charles remained silent. He went on with a resigned sigh. "I called on Clive Merton over at Gidding Constabulary yesterday morning—on another matter, nothing to do with Tony Manners. However, while I was there I made a few discreet inquiries about her." His eyes widened a little. "She used to be a W.P.C. over in Lymstead. Did you know that?"

Mrs. Charles shook her head. "When was this?"

"About ten or eleven years ago. It was only for a short time, then she cracked up under the strain. My impression was that it wasn't entirely the job that got her down. She was caring for her father even then. Anyway, she had a fairly serious nervous breakdown and was in and out of various hospitals over a long period and finally had to resign from the force. She finished up spending almost a year getting herself together again in a place called The Grange over in Lymstead, run by some weirdo faith healer."

Mrs. Charles nodded and said, "Rosa Trumble."

"Oh." David sounded disappointed. "You know about her."

"Yes, but unfortunately my inquiries in that direction came to an abrupt full stop."

It was David's turn to nod. "The local authority closed the place down, and Rosa Trumble legged it to Australia."

"Legged it? Does that mean she left in a hurry?"

"No, not really. Just my little joke. I don't think she ever actually did anyone any harm. As far as I can see, her one and only mistake was that, like you, Madame, she didn't conform. And that sort of thing just doesn't sit too well with local authorities, good results or not! As a matter of fact, if it comes down to a choice, failure through conformity is to be preferred over and above success through nonconformity every time."

"So I've noticed," said the clairvoyante. She was quiet for a moment. Then she went on, "So Tony Manners, in setting up as a private inquiry agent, was not living out a fantasy and playing at being a detective, but doing the only kind of work she'd been trained for. I daresay it would've been highly unlikely that the police force would've taken her back after she'd regained her health."

"She would've had no hope, I'd say. Not with a history of mental instability. That would've been a rope round her neck for the rest of her working life."

"Yes, that was what Jimmy Valentine said," mused the clairvoyante out loud.

"Ah," said David with a small smile. "The mysterious sentimental crook." He hesitated, then took the plunge. "He's the dodgy-looking character who was prowling round the village that day, isn't he?" His eyebrows went up. "Friend of yours?"

"Only indirectly. One of Charles the Third's ex–cell mates, I would think. I never asked."

"A burglar?"

She smiled faintly. "I think it might be better if you didn't ask me that particular question, Superintendent."

David studied her for a moment. "You know, that's odd. . . . I mean, if your sentimental Mr. Valentine is a safe-cracker like the bloke in the song. The sergeant who gave me the inside info on Tony Manners reckons her dad used to be a copper—left the force under something of a cloud. Had a bust-up with a superior officer—a chief super by the name of Fullbright. . . . Met the chap once, didn't like him—no one did. Anyway, Manners was apparently tipped off about a big jewel robbery, and he refused to reveal his source. The chap I was talking to was a bit guarded about it, but I gathered there were rumours that Manners himself was suspected of being on the payroll and that this was how he came by the information. However," he went on, pausing momentarily and looking at the clairvoyante steadily, "in the light of your Mr. Valentine's sentimentality over Manners's daughter, one can't help wondering if he wasn't Manners's nark. Valentine might feel indebted to the girl for her father's silence on his account."

Mrs. Charles nodded thoughtfully. Then she said, "That name you mentioned a moment ago, Mr. Manners's superior officer . . ."

"Fullbright, Martin Fullbright. What about him?"

"I was talking to a Mr. Fullbright today over in Lymstead —an elderly gentleman. He was pottering about in the grounds of a private infants school."

"That doesn't sound much like the Fullbright I met. He was a foul-tempered old devil."

"Old?"

"He'd be getting on now. Over seventy. I believe he was coming up for retirement when I met him." David paused reflectively. "That was about ten or so years ago. Quite a time. I don't know if you remember it—the Pym murder trial?" He raised his eyebrows. "Rendell Pym the T.V. actor? He stood trial for the murder of his young wife. Fullbright was the officer in charge of the murder investigation. I went over to Lymstead to see Fullbright about a man and a woman who were involved in a hit-and-run accident in Gidding and whom he thought might be material witnesses in the Pym case. It turned out they weren't the couple he was after so it all came to a dead end—" He broke off and looked at Mrs. Charles intently. "I'm telling you a lot more than I think I am, aren't I?"

"I'm not sure, Superintendent." She was silent for a moment. Then, "I keep stumbling across the same things, the same people. To begin with, it was the Lymstead Spiritualists' Society and then Rosa Trumble, who was a member of that society, and now Rendell Pym, a murderer."

David was shaking his head.

"Pym was acquitted. The Appeal Court quashed his sentence just under a year after his trial."

"Oh?" She looked at him curiously. "I didn't know that."

David shrugged. "Not to put too fine a point on it, there was reasonable doubt about his guilt—thanks largely to the cock-up Fullbright made of the case. Fullbright coerced one of the witnesses—a publican by the name of Purdie, a good friend of Pym's. They trained at the Royal Academy of Dramatic Art together, though only Pym made the grade as an actor. Initially, Purdie looked like being the chief witness for the defence—he gave Pym a cast-iron alibi, said Pym was drinking in his pub at the time of Mrs. Pym's murder. Purdie was very clear on the time because of a fairly heated argument that took place in the public bar when Pym objected to a man and a woman bringing a dog onto the premises with them. The man and woman were on a motoring holiday and were never traced—and never came forward voluntarily (in my opinion, because they were married, but not to each other). Anyway, after the trial, Pym's solicitor kept at Purdie and eventually got the man to admit that under the threat of losing his liquor licence on some trumped-up charge, Fullbright had got him to change his original story and alter the time of the trouble in the bar over the dog by an hour. Which put Pym right in the house with his wife at the time of her death and got him his original guilty verdict. Not that his appeal did him much good. He went stark staring raving mad, you know. They said he was playacting at the trial—feigning insanity—when he raved and ranted at the judge after sentence had been passed. They dragged him from the court cursing and swearing they'd never get the hangman's noose round his neck. . . ."

Mrs. Charles stared at him. "But surely the death penalty had long since been abolished?"

"You couldn't tell Pym that. He'd gone bonkers by this time. Or was pretending to be mad." David hesitated, frowned. "Immediately prior to the murder, he'd been on a tour of the provinces with a play about a man sentenced to death by hanging for the murder of his wife, and right throughout his own trial, Pym played the part of that character. So the prosecuting counsel claimed. It was a devil of a case, Madame. A farce from beginning to end. I was only on the periphery of it—because of the couple involved in the Gidding accident—but I remember being thankful that it wasn't on my patch."

"Where is Pym now, Superintendent?"

He shrugged. "Lord knows. He was finished, of course, as far as his career was concerned. He was in that T.V. soap opera that got the chop a couple of years back—the one set in a Welsh mining community. He was written out of the series the moment he was charged with murder—killed off in a pit disaster. His bosses never even had the decency to wait and see if he were found guilty or not. As a matter of fact, it was this sort of bias that I believe eventually turned the tide in Pym's favour when it came to an appeal. There's no doubt about it, the press, the T.V. moguls, the family doctor, Fullbright—even the judge in his summing up— were all heavily biased against Pym, and guilty or not (and I for one believe he was guilty), he had a right to a fair trial."

He paused, waiting for the clairvoyante to speak. After a minute or two, she said musingly, "It's a long shot, Superintendent, but do you think you could get me a list of everyone involved in Pym's trial—including anybody the police might have interviewed in connection with their inquiries?" She hesitated. Then she said meditatively, "I don't suppose you'd remember if Benjamin Bing was a witness at Pym's trial?"

"Our spiritualist friend?" David shook his head. "No, I'd remember him."

"I wonder why Tony really went to see him?"

"You don't think it had anything to do with her being depressed over the state of her health?"

Mrs. Charles hesitated before replying. Then, in a slow, thoughtful voice, "Admittedly Rosa Trumble was in Australia—Tony could hardly seek help from her—and Bing was close at hand. But this would then mean that Tony was aware of his reputation as a faith healer, and my feeling is that she knew nothing of his healing powers until she picked up the *Sketch* in the Half Moon Cafe that morning—the day she died—and read about the death of Mr. Justice Halahan. . . . Yes, Superintendent," she interpolated with a slow nod, "*that* Mr. Justice Halahan—the so-called 'hanging judge,' who heard Rendell Pym's case and who, himself, died as a result of a hanging accident. And while Benjamin Bing's powers of healing might have greatly interested Tony—and it is by no means certain that she was the hypochondriac everyone would seem to wish to paint her—I don't think she was the kind of person to rush headlong into something. She would've made a few discreet inquiries first, then gone quietly over to Lymstead to see Bing about her problem." She paused, sighed. Then, slowly shaking her head, she said, "I don't know—there are just too many coincidences."

"I've seen some pretty remarkable ones in my time. It's best not to read too much into anything concerning the girl until you've got something more concrete," he advised. "The evidence at the inquest was pretty overwhelming where Bing was concerned—I've checked. I think you'll find she went to see him about her health."

"Then what was he afraid of, Superintendent?"

"Who? Bing?"

She nodded. "I understand he was reduced almost to a gibbering wreck when he was called to give evidence at the inquest."

"Maybe he's a sensitive soul."

"Perhaps," said Mrs. Charles. But she sounded far from convinced.

CHAPTER NINE

Mrs. Charles stood at the window and watched David drive away. Was he right? Was she reading too much into things? Wasn't this a simple, straightforward instance of an emotionally unstable young woman, neurotically concerned about her health, picking up a newspaper one morning and chancing upon a new avenue to explore and then, on discovering that it led nowhere, taking her life in a fit of despondency?

Mrs. Charles frowned. No. Follow that path and she would finish up with the same conclusions that everyone else had reached (she was more than halfway there already!). To arrive at the truth she should divorce herself completely from all supposition associated with Tony Manners's health, both the time of her death and previous to it, and concentrate on the one and only concrete fact she had to go on, the case Tony Manners had been investigating when she had died.

"Mrs. Dolly Dackers (bird fancier/spurned woman), formerly of Uppingham, now of Lymstead," murmured the clairvoyante, "versus Mr. Neville Krendel (pet shop proprietor/dog hater) of Gidding."

Mrs. Charles's frown deepened. Now why, she asked herself, keep two separate files on what was presumably the same case? One file in the office—the one the police had found (and to which Jimmy Valentine had referred and which had apparently contained no specific mention of Neville Krendel, or Jimmy Valentine would have said something about him)—and the other in a safe at her flat (this one containing a slip of paper with Neville Krendel's name on it and mention of at least one breed of bird that Mimi Laffont could remember, the finch), which Mimi Laffont and her sister were instructed to destroy should anything happen to Tony.

Because there was not one, but two cases under investigation involving the same parties? The investigation Tony was carrying out under instructions from Mrs. Dackers on behalf of the consortium of bird fanciers she headed and the other involving Neville Krendel (and therefore presumably Mrs. Dackers). But under instructions this time from whom? Dolly Dackers again? Someone else?

Mrs. Charles shook her head slowly and turned from the window. Then, suddenly, she paused.

Tony herself? Was this the explanation for the file kept safely hidden away from prying eyes at home? Was Tony— for some personal reason—carrying out an investigation of her own into Neville Krendel and his business activities?

But if Tony had kept that edition of the *Sketch* for June tenth because of the item on the bird thefts, it had to be the same case. So why leave instructions for the whole file to be destroyed in the event of her death? Surely if her death and that file were in any way linked—and Tony suspected that her life was at risk because of these inquiries of her own—it would be vital that the file should reach the hands of the police.

Or had Tony known that this would never happen, that the landlord of her business premises, Ernest Hammond, would react to the news of her death precisely as he had and contrive to get inside her flat ahead of the police and remove the file? Or was it someone else Tony was worried about? Jimmy Valentine? Had she known that in the event of her death, he would break into her office to gain access to her files? Could this have been the reason for the secret file?

Mrs. Charles spent several minutes considering both this and the further possibility that she was being used for a purpose very far removed from the one Jimmy Valentine had given her, then switched her thoughts back to the estate agent for a moment. She had met Ernest Hammond once, very briefly, when she had bought her present home, The

Bungalow. His firm had handled the sale. Her only recollection of him was that he was elderly (well past retiring age then she would have said), bald, portly and vague to the point of senility in all matters excepting monetary ones, which sharply concentrated his mind—almost as if at the flick of a switch, she recalled with a wry smile.

She couldn't say that his firm's business dealings with her had been in any way unscrupulous or unfair, and she knew there would be few landlords of any kind of substandard property who would treat their tenants any better than he had Tony Manners. It would be naive to think otherwise. That wasn't the way men like Ernest Hammond got to be wealthy landlords.

With a sigh, Mrs. Charles admitted to herself that she was up against the same blank wall the police had found when they had investigated Tony Manners's death. For once it was of no use to her to have uncovered something they had missed—not without having the actual file itself—which left her, as they had been, with only Tony's possible state of mind on the day of her death as an explanation.

"Full circle," murmured the clairvoyante. Back where she began . . . With a registered faith healer, Benjamin Bing, and the curious fact (though possibly this was quite coincidental) that no matter where her inquiries took her, at some point along the way passing reference would be made either to the Lymstead Spiritualists' Society or to one or more of its members.

She thought for a moment or two about the society's meeting which she planned to attend the following Tuesday night. She couldn't help feeling that it was the only door left open to her.

The guest speaker at the Tuesday evening meeting of the combined Gidding and Lymstead Spiritualists' societies was not Mr. John Ramsay, the late Mr. Justice Halahan's butler (as had been advertised in the *Sketch* the previous week), but a Canadian spiritualist who attended the meeting unexpectedly and whom John Ramsay had graciously agreed to step down for when requested so to do by the president of both societies, Benjamin Bing.

Ramsay and an attractive brunette in her late thirties quietly laid out chunky white cups and saucers while the visitor gave his talk, Ramsay moving with a respectful deferentiality to the guest speaker backwards and forwards between the locker where the tea things were kept and the trestle table on which he and his lady helper were preparing supper. The president had fussily apologised for the need for this while the talk was in progress and explained that the society had the hire of the hall only until ten-thirty and that the caretaker was most strict about their vacating the premises on or before that hour.

Mrs. Charles had not been introduced to Ramsay, nor had he been singled out in any way from the remaining handful of male spiritualists present at the meeting other than by name when the president had mounted the platform to introduce their Canadian visitor and referred to Ramsay's deferred talk, and yet there was no doubt at all in the clairvoyante's mind that this man preparing the supper would be the late Mr. Justice Halahan's butler.

Ramsay was wearing tweeds, but even in swimming trunks John Ramsay would not have been able to get away from what he was. "Butler to the gentry" was stamped all over him—in the autocratic way he held his head, in his youthfully graceful, swift, and silent movements, in the total lack of expression with its promise of absolute discretion in any circumstances. Were it not for the extreme whiteness of his hair, Mrs. Charles would have put his age at somewhere between fifty and sixty.

As for Benjamin Bing, he was a soft-spoken, slightly built man in his late sixties, whose quiet aura of self-control struck the clairvoyante as being a deliberate pose to mask a frustrated, highly strung, nervous individual. Only the faintest of smiles disturbed his pale, tense features when he thanked her after the talk for attending the meeting. He added that he and his members also sincerely hoped it would be the first of many such visits and that she must stay and enjoy a cup of tea with them. He then went on to apologise for the small attendance that night, which he blamed in part on the weather, which was wet and stormy.

". . . And so many of our members are on holiday at this time of year," he continued with a tremulous smile of thanks for the herbal tea which Ramsay's helper had brought him. He looked around to see what was being done about refreshments for Mrs. Charles, but Ramsay's helper had her back to him and was talking to the Canadian visitor. After a moment, Mr. Bing went on.

"Have you been interested in spiritualism for long, um, Mrs.—?" He hesitated. "I'm sorry, I didn't quite catch your name. I'm a little hard of hearing."

"Charles," replied the clairvoyante. "Edwina Charles."

As Mrs. Charles spoke, Mr. Bing looked round again to see what was keeping Ramsay's helper, but she had disappeared. He made a small sign to Ramsay, who filled a cup from a huge dented aluminium teapot and brought it over to the clairvoyante.

"I understand you've had a great deal of success with the treatment of severe migraine headaches," remarked the clairvoyante as Ramsay returned to his post in charge of the teapot.

Mr. Bing looked bemused.

"You are the gentleman who treated Mr. Justice Halahan and Antonia Manners for headaches, aren't you? I read about you in the *Sketch*."

Mrs. Charles thought for a moment that the spiritual healer was going to faint. His expression became glacial; his whole body tensed. Then, curiously, he smiled. Only it wasn't a real smile, more a reflex action promoted by extreme tension. Plus something else. Fear? wondered the clairvoyante.

"A terrible tragedy," he remarked at length in his soft

voice. His pale blue eyes blinked at her through his rimless spectacles. "Most distressing."

"I suppose you were inundated with inquiries from migraine sufferers as a result of the mention in the *Sketch*."

"No, not really. One or two people contacted me at the time." He paused, then blinked again in the same slow, piteous way. "And now you, of course," he added softly.

Mrs. Charles said, "I was a little surprised when I heard that Tony Manners had consulted you. But then I didn't realise that Mrs. Trumble had emigrated to Australia, which, of course, explained everything."

Mr. Bing looked at her blankly.

"Tony was actually one of Mrs. Trumble's patients, wasn't she?"

"A remarkable woman," said Mr. Bing. "We were very sorry about her."

"Miss Manners, Tony?"

"Mrs. Trumble. She was both our president and our resident healer. I filled the breach when she left. I barely knew Miss Manners. In fact, I only saw her that one time."

"She never attended any of your meetings?" Mrs. Charles looked surprised. "Not even while Mrs. Trumble was president?"

"No, never. To the best of my knowledge, Miss Manners was not a spiritualist."

"Oh," said Mrs. Charles. She paused. Then, "How odd. I naturally assumed she was once a member of the Lymstead Spiritualists' Society or at least that she had leanings your way through her association with Rosa Trumble. Perhaps I misunderstood. A mutual friend of Tony's and mine told me that Tony made a deliberate point of contacting you after she'd read about Mr. Justice Halahan's death because—"

Again Mr. Bing looked as if he were going to faint. His whole body stiffened, swayed. Then, abruptly, the strange, nervous little smile was back on his lips. "Forgive me," he said, "but I really must excuse myself for a few moments and have a word with our Canadian visitor before he leaves. I have enjoyed meeting you. You will come again, won't you?"

He glided smoothly away, controlled as ever, without waiting for the clairvoyante's reply. She did not know how Mr. Bing had earned a living prior to his retirement (she presumed he was retired, that spirit healing had not always been his principal source of income), but she was prepared to make a guess. The care with which he chose his words and phrased his consistently evasive replies to her questions suggested that he had been either a lawyer (or engaged in an occupation which was closely connected with the legal profession) or he had been in banking—a bank manager's clerk, perhaps, whose task it had been discreetly but firmly to ward off any unwelcome advances made by customers in his immediate superior's direction.

CHAPTER TEN

Mrs. Charles introduced herself to John Ramsay when she returned her cup to the table. She was saved the need for any further explanations. Ramsay responded to the mention of her name immediately with a polite expression of pleasure at having finally met her.

"We are all well aware, Madame," he went on, "both here in Gidding and at our sister church in Lymstead, of your work. We speak of you often and the good you do our cause. I am quite sure our Mr. Bing has personally expressed his delight at your presence here tonight."

Mrs. Charles considered Ramsay thoughtfully. So even here Benjamin Bing was being careful by not owning that he was aware that she was a clairvoyante.

"I wonder, Mr. Ramsay," she said, "if I might have a private word with you?"

"Certainly, Madame," he said dutifully, as if she had asked him to fetch madam the newspapers or some other item that her ladyship wanted.

He picked up his tea, and they moved back against the wall away from the table.

Mrs. Charles went on. "I was just speaking with Mr. Bing about Mr. Justice Halahan."

"Yes," he said, his tone singularly lacking a questioning note.

"He still seems very distressed about it," she remarked.

"Mr. Bing was with Mr. Justice Halahan for many years," said Ramsay.

Mrs. Charles looked at him. "Mr. Bing was a member of his household staff?"

"Oh no, Madame. Mr. Bing is a lawyer. He was Mr. Justice Halahan's clerk."

Mrs. Charles hesitated. Then, slowly, "At the time of the Pym murder trial?"

"Yes, Madame. Mr. Bing was with Mr. Justice Halahan for over twenty years."

There was a small, thoughtful pause. Then Mrs. Charles asked, "Were you with the judge at the time of that trial?"

"Yes, Madame, I was. I became butler to Mr. Justice Halahan in 1934, and with the exception of a few years during the last war when Beechbrook—Mr. Justice Halahan's family home—and its staff, including myself, were requisitioned by the Ministry of Defence for the war effort, I was with him right up until his death."

Mrs. Charles was quiet for a moment. Then, in a thoughtful voice, she said, "It was an interesting case. Though most distressing, I should imagine, from the judge's point of view."

Ramsay looked at her. "In what way would that be, Madame?"

Mrs. Charles's eyebrows rose. "Pym's histrionic outburst from the dock as he was being sentenced? I'm sure Mr. Justice Halahan found that most disturbing."

"No, Madame, I wouldn't have said so. It would have been all in a day's work for Mr. Justice Halahan. Rendell Pym was not the first during his years on the bench to issue such a threat. It used to be said of Pym—the roles in which he was usually cast—that he was the man everyone loved to hate, and I think it would be fairly safe to say that as an accomplished, highly successful actor, he made the most of his situation and played his role as a brutal wife killer to the hilt. Nobody, I am sure, took the threats he made to the lives of everybody who had spoken out against him seriously. That was only the actor, not the man speaking."

"Did Mr. Justice Halahan ever express his views on the decision of the Appeal Court to set aside Pym's sentence?"

"He felt, Madame, that there had been a grave miscarriage of justice, but he accepted the findings of his peers in the proper spirit, that is to say, in the manner befitting his position."

"But he always held Pym to be guilty of the murder for which he was tried?"

"Yes, Madame. That is my belief, although he never expressed that view to me personally."

"I see." The clairvoyante paused. Then, after a moment, "Please forgive my impertinence, but might I ask if he ever expressed to you his thoughts about Pym's character?"

"Yes, Madame. He thought Pym was a callous, cold-hearted swine," said the butler without a trace of emotion. "As indeed did I and a great many other people who followed Pym's trial. He was an extremely unpleasant, thoroughly offensive fellow. Though, as is so often the case, the Good Lord works in mysterious ways, and I am pleased to be able to say that before the day eventually came for Rendell Pym to meet his Maker, he was a completely reformed character."

Mrs. Charles gave Ramsay an interested look. "You knew Rendell Pym personally?"

"No, Madame, Pym and I never met. In the circumstances, my being in the employ of Mr. Justice Halahan, that would not have been seemly."

The clairvoyante eyed him shrewdly. "But you nevertheless know what became of Pym after he was freed."

"Yes, Madame. Approximately eighteen months after his sentence was set aside, Pym suffered a serious mental breakdown and was nursed back to health (though thereafter he was, I understand, only a shadow of the man he was before) by one of our former members, Mrs. Rosa Trumble, who was matron of a small nursing home in Lymstead. Pym spent the remaining years of his life—this was after he had recovered his senses—tending the nursing home's vegetable garden and looking after the grounds."

"I have heard that Mrs. Trumble was a remarkable woman."

"Yes, Madame. She had a natural gift for healing which the authorities, I am sorry to say, considered too unorthodox, and eventually they felt obliged to close down the home. Mrs. Trumble was getting on in years, and like every other hospital in the country, her home was packed to capacity—an enormous responsibility for her. So I don't think the closure came as too much of a blow to her. Something of a relief, I've always thought, especially as her daughter needed her. Mrs. Trumble's daughter had emigrated to Australia with her husband and family, and there was some problem with one of the youngest grandchildren, who was sickly. There was apparently nothing more the doctors could do for the child, and it was hoped that once again Mrs. Trumble's divine gift for healing would prevail and the child's life would be spared."

Mrs. Charles nodded slowly. Then, after a brief pause, she asked, "Do you recall when Pym died?"

"Not the exact date, Madame. But it would have been somewhere around the time of the closure of Mrs. Trumble's nursing home, which must be something like two years ago. I recall Mrs. Trumble's brother dropping in to one of our Lymstead meetings with news of Mrs. Trumble and the sick grandchild, and he mentioned Pym's—"

Ramsay's helper suddenly came up and touched him lightly on the sleeve of his jacket. Then, smiling at him, she said, "You're having such a nice chat with our visitor, John. I'll do the dishes and clear up tonight."

Ramsay thanked her and gave up his cup and saucer. He was wearing a hairpiece, Mrs. Charles noted as he turned his head to speak to the other woman. It wasn't noticeable from the front, but at the back of his head, where the hairpiece met his own rather coarse hair, it tended to lay across his scalp like a thick white rug.

"You were saying?" said the clairvoyante as the other woman tiptoed away.

Ramsay hesitated. "I don't think there was anything more I was going to say, Madame."

Mrs. Charles went back to the point they had reached immediately prior to their interruption in the hope that, by so doing, Ramsay would suddenly recollect what he had been going to say about Pym.

"Rendell Pym died, you said, about two years ago?"

"Yes, Madame. That is correct."

"Was Mr. Justice Halahan aware of this?"

"No, Madame. My employer eventually heard about Pym's suicide while having a telephone conversation with a New Zealand author who was seeking an interview with him about Pym's trial. I purposely never brought up the matter myself, though Mr. Justice Halahan did make some comment in passing, but only to express his surprise that Pym had been living incognito in the district for so many years."

"You never told him of Pym's return to the Lymstead area soon after his release from prison?"

"No, Madame. I did not think that would be wise."

Mrs. Charles's eyes widened interrogatively. "You feared the revelation of Pym's whereabouts might have distressed him?"

"No, Madame. That would not have distressed him anywhere near as much as my interest in spiritualism."

The clairvoyante gave him another questioning look.

"Mr. Justice Halahan would not have approved, Madame. And in telling him about one, I would've undoubtedly had to make some mention of the other. It was only quite recently that Mr. Justice Halahan came to spiritualism."

"Ah yes," said Mrs. Charles, nodding. "His headaches . . ." She hesitated. Then, "I wonder, Mr. Ramsay, if I might ask another impertinent question?" She paused, and he inclined his head a fraction to one side in what she assumed to be a gesture of acquiescence. "It's about your employer's headaches. . . ."

Ramsay made no comment. He waited for her to continue.

"Did he suffer depression with these attacks of migraine?" she inquired.

Ramsay studied her for a moment before replying. "Occasionally, Madame. Though more often than not, the attacks would come on after a period, which could sometimes last several days, of extreme hyperactivity and excitement."

"Was he depressed on the day of his accident?"

"No, Madame. Excited. At least, that was his frame of mind shortly before lunch, which was the last time I was to see him until I returned home late that night and found him near death in his bedroom. Mr. Janus—the author of whom I spoke a few minutes ago—also commented on his high spirits that day. They lunched together—had what I believe is commonly termed 'a working lunch'—in the library."

"They were discussing the Pym trial?"

"Yes, Madame. Mr. Justice Halahan had agreed to assist Mr. Janus with his research on Pym and the trial in any way he could. Mr. Janus and I were the last people to see Mr. Justice Halahan alive."

Mrs. Charles looked at him thoughtfully. "Was there no other member of the domestic staff in the house that day?"

"Mrs. Keogh, the housekeeper, had returned—it was her day off as well—but Mr. Justice Halahan had retired for the night by then. She simply cleared away the lunch things from the library and then went straight up to bed."

"Mr. Justice Halahan and the author lunched alone?"

"Yes, Madame. Mr. Janus left the house at around three-thirty in the afternoon and returned to the hotel in Gidding where he was staying prior to his return to London the next morning. He was most distressed when the police contacted him and told him what had happened, particularly as Mr. Justice Halahan had, he said, been in such a cheerful frame of mind. But then, Mr. Janus is himself getting on in years and rather frail, I understand."

Something stirred in the back of Mrs. Charles's mind. She tried to think what it was, but she couldn't remember. Slowly, she said, "He didn't give evidence at the inquest?"

"No, Madame. He made a statement to the police and was excused. There was no need for him to attend."

"I see," she said. There was a long pause, then she asked, "Do you think you could let me have the address of Mrs. Trumble's brother?"

"I'm sorry, Madame, but I don't know what became of the gentleman after the closing down of the nursing home. He had, in effect, lost his own home with its closure—that is to say, he would have done, eventually (I believe he agreed to remain on at the home for a few weeks as caretaker until the local authority had decided on its future). And when he called in on us that night, he said he was contemplating joining his sister in Australia. Though whether he did or not I cannot say. Mrs. Dackers might possibly know—the lady who came up and spoke to me a few minutes ago. She was a close friend of Mrs. Trumble's."

The clairvoyante looked at him meditatively. "Mrs. Dolly Dackers?"

"Yes, Madame. Mrs. Dackers and Mrs. Trumble were the cofounder members of the Lymstead Spiritualists' Society."

CHAPTER ELEVEN

It was after listening to the ten o'clock newscast on television that ex-Detective Chief Superintendent Martin Fullbright decided to go out for his evening walk with his dog.

The storm had passed and the rain had stopped, but it was quite chilly now and so he put on a raincoat. There was probably more rain about, anyway, he decided, despite what they had promised in the weather report, and there was no sense in getting a soaking.

He groped about in the stair cupboard for his walking stick and then whistled sharply. He listened for a moment, head cocked, then whistled again. *Where was that dratted dog?* "Here, Blackie!" he called irritably and whistled again.

The hall was in darkness, so Fullbright couldn't see the animal, whose colouring had been the unimaginative inspiration for its name. But Fullbright could hear his low growl.

Now what was the matter with him tonight? Fullbright wondered with a frown. He'd been rumbling away at the back of his throat like that all day. Could dogs really tell when something was wrong, sense when something bad was going to happen?

Fullbright considered the possibility. Wasn't that accrediting an animal with supernatural powers?

"What's up with you?" he asked the dog gruffly. "The arthritis bothering you, eh? Well, welcome to the club!"

The dog responded with another low growl.

"Well," said Fullbright impatiently. "Are you coming or aren't you? Make up your mind!"

The dog thought about it for a moment and then made his decision, allowing his lead to be clipped onto his collar, though his hackles were slightly raised and another growl was bubbling in his throat.

"What is it, eh?" asked Fullbright. "Something's worrying you, isn't it? Mice—is that it? Can you hear mice in the skirting boards again? What say we get ourselves a randy old tom and let him worry about them, eh?"

Fullbright chuckled and together—the dog still grumbling—they stepped out into the night.

Ellen Purdie opened the door of the public bar just wide enough to give her a glimpse of the street beyond. The Ugly Duckling's forecourt shone like black patent leather after the heavy rain shower, which had deluged Lymstead shortly before closing time at ten-thirty, and the night air smelt fresh and sweet. Intermittent rain drops, the tail end of the passing shower, dimpled the puddles which lay about everywhere. But the landlord's stepdaughter noticed none of these things.

She frowned to herself. They were still out there, skylarking about under the lamppost on the other side of the road. They'd had far too much to drink, and she wished her father had turned them out of the bar much sooner than he had. They were all friends of Trev's, but fortunately her father hadn't realised that: she would never have heard the end of it if he had.

Her heart gave a sudden lurch as she recognised the fourth male figure, who sauntered up to join the three youths near the lamppost, and she quickly closed the door and shot the bolts.

"They still hanging about out there?" her father called to her from the rear of the premises.

The sound of shattering glass as an empty beer bottle went flying across the road and smashed to smithereens against the far kerb obliterated the first half of her reply. "Please don't go out there, Dad," she added. "They'll go in a minute."

Purdie appeared at the back of the bar and began to roll

down his shirt sleeves over his hairy forearms, which looked vaguely damp and shiny. Ellen watched him a little fearfully and wondered where he had been in the fifteen minutes which had elapsed since his seeing the young men off the premises; but she didn't ask.

Crossing to the door, Purdie drew back the bolts and said, "See you lock up properly after me. I'll come in the back way after I've taken care of them."

Ellen's heart raced madly. She followed him to the door, trying to think of something to say, anything that would stop him going out of that door and finding Trevor Flegg with the other three lads, but her tongue and throat muscles were tied up in a hard knot of fear and she couldn't make herself speak.

She heard him bellowing at the young men to move on or he would fetch the police: then, through a crack in the door, she watched Trevor Flegg. Colour flooded her face. He was staring moodily at the ground and beginning to paw at it with his scruffy gym shoes like a small, truculent boy. There was going to be trouble. Her father had scared the other lads with his threat of calling out the police, but not Trev.

One of the smaller lads was protesting in a shrill voice that they were waiting for a bus to take them home; and her father bawled back at him, making a series of threatening gestures with his thick right arm and a clenched fist, to go and wait somewhere else.

There was a pause, a perfect stillness, and Ellen held her breath. She had seen situations like this before. This was the critical moment. If any real unpleasantness was going to take place, it would happen now or never.

She let out her breath in a long sigh as all four lads capitulated and moved off sulkily down the road. Quickly, before her father could turn round and catch her watching him, she shut the door and locked and bolted it again. Then she switched out all the lights in the bar and went into the back room to count the evening's takings.

Purdie waited until the lads had turned the corner and disappeared. Muttering to himself about the youth of today and what he would and would not do about the increase in juvenile crime given half a chance, he started back across the forecourt, pausing to scowl at some broken glass (if he had noticed *that* before he would have made them sweep it up before he had sent them on their way!). Then, after picking up the larger pieces of glass and dispersing the rest with the sole of his shoe, he went down the side of the public house.

A cat streaked past him, screeching as he caught the side of one of the dustbins with his right foot, and he cursed it irritably, hesitating briefly to drop the broken glass in the bin and then replace its lid, which the cat had dislodged in its startled flight.

He rounded the corner of the building. Then, as he started up the short flight of steps to the back door, he heard a noise at the dustbins again, and he looked about him quickly for something to throw at the stray, which he assumed had returned and recommenced its foraging the moment he had turned his back. There was an old broom standing against the wall near the door and he settled for that, grabbing it up and then creeping back on tiptoe across the rear of the premises and peeping cautiously round the corner.

The dustbin, the one whose lid he had replaced, was lying on its side lidless, its contents spewed everywhere. So great was his annoyance at the mess which he would now have to clear up that it did not occur to him to wonder where the scrawny stray had found the necessary strength to overturn the three-quarters full, heavy galvanised-iron rubbish receptacle.

He left the broom leaning against the side wall and then stooped down to right the dustbin. Wheezing a little, more with bad temper than because he was out of breath, he began to replace the rubbish. He had almost finished tidying up when he sensed rather than actually heard someone moving stealthily behind him. Flegg, he thought. He straightened up and swung round defensively, all a little too quickly after having been bent almost double for some minutes.

The blood drained from his head, and spots swam before his eyes. He closed them tightly, only very briefly but long enough for his attacker to deal him one hefty blow to the side of the head.

With his arms raised to fend off any successive blows, Purdie fell grunting to his knees. Blood trickled into his left eye and he tried to blink it away. His head felt numb, and he knew that while he could not feel any real pain, the mere fact that there was this awful numbness indicated that he was badly hurt.

For a few moments everything went black, then his vision cleared and he looked up at the figure towering menacingly above him. Giddiness and nausea washed over him in wave after wave. He blinked away the blood again, and for a fleeting, bewildered instant the blurred features of his assailant cleared and he saw his face distinctly.

Purdie thought he uttered his killer's name, but he didn't: it died with him, a shriek in his brain, as a second, fatal blow was delivered with vicious accuracy to the crown of his head, crushing it.

CHAPTER TWELVE

Mrs. Charles opened the door and considered the bemused expression on her caller's face.

"You've been visiting the Laffont sisters," David Sayer greeted her challengingly.

"So?" she said.

"It's true?" He followed the clairvoyante into her sitting room. "You know who they are, don't you?"

"Yes, Tony Manners's landladies."

"Oh," he said. Then, after a small pause, "Well, that should take the wind out of Clive Merton's sails, anyway. I've never seen a man laugh so hard. He thought it was a huge joke when one of the uniformed chaps reported that he suspected the Laffonts were recruiting a new girl and your name was mentioned. Especially as it was the extracurricular activities of the two young French students in the upstairs flat that everybody was worried about. You saw the sign in the window, didn't you? The one about the French lessons?" He chuckled. "Nothing anyone can do about it, of course, but everybody knows what's really going on in there. They've been at it for years. For as long as I can remember, anyway." He paused, grinning. Then, reaching into his pocket, he took out a folded sheet of notepaper, opened it out, and then handed it to her. "Your list of names, Madame," he explained. "With maybe one additional surprise I'll tell you about later."

Mrs. Charles began to read from the list out loud.

"Dr. Angus MacDonald . . ."

David said, "Mrs. Pym's doctor. He gave quite damning evidence at the trial on the appalling bruising he observed all over her body at various times. Pym regularly beat her up. She'd just turned twenty-one when he killed her. He was in his late thirties."

Mrs. Charles thought for a moment, nodded. Then, continuing with the list, "Neville Krendel."

"Mrs. Pym's lover," said David. "One of them, according to Pym. Krendel lodged next door with the woman named next on the list, Mrs. Finch. Pym swore it was Krendel who killed his wife, but Mrs. Finch alibied him. Months later she retracted her statement and admitted she'd lied about Krendel being up in his room at the time of the murder. This new statement was made after Purdie, the publican, had confessed to Pym's lawyer that Fullbright had pressured him into giving false evidence. Krendel was never accused of the crime—formally charged, that is. The evidence against him was too circumstantial. And in any event, as far as the police were concerned, they were one hundred percent convinced they were right the first time."

Mrs. Charles nodded slowly. "Mrs. D. Finch," she read out loud from the list. Then, looking up at David, "What does the *D* stand for?"

"Doris, I believe."

Mrs. Charles's eyebrows went up. "Sometimes known as Dolly?" she wondered aloud. Then, "I don't suppose you'd happen to know if this Mrs. Finch breeds birds?"

David smiled. "I don't know about breeding them, but in her original statement to the police, she claimed the fight it was generally believed Pym had with his wife the night he killed her disturbed some birds she kept in an outside aviary."

Mrs. Charles thought for a moment, then looked again at the list.

"Hammond," she said.

"Big-noise estate agent in town—Gidding, that is," said David. "Ex-town councillor, ex-mayor—you've probably heard of him. He's filthy rich—owns half of Gidding and a goodly slice of Lymstead—and he's mean with it. And a known womaniser. He owned the house the Pyms were renting. At his trial, Pym claimed Hammond was one of the men his wife was sleeping around with while he was away on tour, but he was never able to prove it. However, Hammond's name was later found in a diary of names and dates belonging to Mrs. Pym, which Mrs. Finch claimed she'd found in Krendel's room. (None of this, of course, came out until Purdie—the publican—finally admitted that he'd perjured himself to save his liquor licence.) Anyway, when the police eventually tackled Krendel about the diary, he admitted that he went in to see Mrs. Pym that night—the night she was killed—but he claimed she was already dead. He said he found her lying in a pool of blood on the kitchen floor and he panicked, cleared out of there as fast as he could, taking the diary—which he said was on the floor beside her body—because his name (along with the names of all the other men in Mrs. Pym's life) was in it.

"Krendel, it seems, was a busy chap," David continued with a wry smile. "He was Mrs. Finch's lover too as well as being her lodger, and it was after Mrs. Finch caught him playing fast and loose with another party, apparently, that she handed over the diary she claimed to have found in his room. Krendel and Mrs. Finch, incidentally, were already known to the police. Mrs. Finch was in the habit of reporting him to them every time they had a row and always on some trumped-up charge. She'd give him permission to use her car and then call up the police and swear he'd stolen it . . . that sort of nonsense. Though not in the instance of Mrs. Pym's diary. That was genuine enough."

Mrs. Charles nodded again, then considered the next name on the list. "Roger Purdie. Yes . . . the publican," she said, passing straight on to the next name. "Martin Fullbright."

"Detective Chief Super," said David. "Pym called him 'the ape.' Sarcastic devil—Pym, that is (and Fullbright, for that matter). The three wise monkeys, Pym called them . . . the doctor, Fullbright, and the judge." He paused.

"The doctor, MacDonald, saw the bruising on Mrs. Pym's body and gave evidence to that effect. That gives us Pym's first wise monkey, see no evil. The third wise monkey who should've spoken no evil ('an unmitigated liar,' the defence lawyer called him) was Fullbright. And the second wise monkey was the judge, Halahan. Hear no evil."

Mrs. Charles looked at him steadily. She spoke quietly. "But why cover only the one ear, Superintendent?"

He stared at her. "I'm not with you, Madame."

"Mr. Justice Halahan was found by his butler hanging from a rope attached to his bedroom curtain rail with one hand—his right one—taped with adhesive plaster to the side of his head. As part of a neck exercise to relieve migraine headaches, the butler believed."

"You think—?" David paused, frowned. He spoke slowly. "I was in Halahan's court once. If I remember rightly, he was completely deaf in one ear and hard-of-hearing in the other. Sat through all of his trials leaning forward on the bench with one hand cupped behind his good ear to encourage witnesses to speak up when they were giving their evidence."

He watched Mrs. Charles get up and cross to the window, where she stood looking out over the rose garden. After a minute or two, she said, "Are you aware that Dr. MacDonald was recently beaten up, robbed, and murdered in a Scottish graveyard and then left by his attackers with his hands taped over his eyes—it was presumed so that he would not be able to identify the person or persons who had attacked him?"

"Who told you this?"

"Mrs. Flegg, Tony's cleaning woman. She used to be Dr. MacDonald's housekeeper over in Lymstead before he retired and went back home to Scotland to live."

David's eyes narrowed. "Did Tony Manners know about what happened to him?"

Mrs. Charles, turning from the window, nodded and said, "That, I am now beginning to think, might have been what she was doing on the night train to Glasgow. Somehow Tony made the connection with the taping of his hands across his eyes with what she had read in the *Sketch* that morning of Halahan's death—the taping of his hand over his ear. She then went out to see Benjamin Bing, who I've now discovered was formerly Halahan's clerk. She probably got nowhere with him—as I did last night when I spoke to him at a spiritualists' meeting in Gidding—so she got on a train to Glasgow to see what she could find out at MacDonald's end." The clairvoyante paused. Then, frowning, "What I don't understand is *how* she made the connection."

"That was the little surprise I've been keeping up my sleeve," said David with a smile. "Tony Manners was involved in the Pym case. Not the actual murder—Fullbright saw the danger there and had her smartly transferred out of the area. Tony Manners was the W.P.C. who went round and dried Mrs. Pym's tears each time Pym came home, either from touring or Wales (where he spent five days a week for the greater part of the year filming the T.V. series I spoke about) and beat her up. Only Tony Manners apparently saw both sides of the coin, so to speak. She knew for a fact that Mrs. Pym wasn't the lily-white angel the prosecution claimed. And as I've said before, Fullbright wanted his conviction. Pym's head on a plate and no one else's. There was no way he was going to let that girl get up on the witness stand and undermine his case by admitting to the defence that Mrs. Pym had a whole regiment of lovers, any one of whom could have killed her."

There was a long pause. Then Mrs. Charles said, "He has to be next, Superintendent. The third and final wise monkey."

"I don't think I follow you, Madame. Next for what?"

"To be killed. Wasn't Pym dragged from court cursing everybody who'd spoken out against him?"

"His ravings were directed mainly, I think, at the judge. I don't know about anybody else. Though Pym was so deranged at the time I daresay he could've meant anybody and everybody connected with his trial, as you've suggested."

"But more than likely the two chief prosecution witnesses who gave evidence against him and the judge who sentenced him."

"Perhaps." David spoke reluctantly. "What d'you suggest? D'you think I should have a word with Merton about this?"

"It might be wise." The clairvoyante hesitated, looking bemused. "But *who*, Superintendent? If I'm right, and something does happen to Martin Fullbright, who is carrying out this vendetta? It can't be Pym himself. He's dead."

David nodded. "Yes. He died two years ago." There was a long silence. Then he said, "I wonder. . . . Do you think the girl could've been on to someone?"

Mrs. Charles sighed heavily. "All I know for certain is that she was carrying out a private investigation of her own—at least, this is how it looks to me—into two people, both of whom it would now seem were deeply involved in one way or another with Rendell Pym and his murdered wife. . . . Mrs. Doris Finch—whom I believe is also known as Dolly Dackers—and Neville Krendel."

The clairvoyante then went on to explain about the file the police had removed from Tony Manners's office in Gidding and the secret one which it now seemed more than likely had involved the same parties and which the Laffont sisters had been instructed to destroy.

"Odd," commented David when she had finished. "Though the instructions she left concerning the second file might only mean that her investigations were still far from complete and she didn't want the file falling into the wrong hands and casting possibly false aspersions on innocent people."

Mrs. Charles said, "Perhaps. It's one explanation for her behaviour that morning when she went dashing off to see Benjamin Bing. She appears to have been a careful girl, slow and, I would've thought, methodical—and, I would also think, highly principled—and yet that day her behaviour was completely out of character. Though not if she believed that she was still a long way off getting whatever answer she sought."

The clairvoyante's eyes narrowed. "Her suspicions, there-fore—whatever they were—must have still been extremely vague, otherwise I'm sure—and having had some formal police training as well as actual experience in the police force—she would've approached Bing with a great deal more caution. There's no doubt in my mind, Superinten-dent, that she died either because she went to see him and someone found out about it (possibly through Tony herself when she talked to someone about where she was going) or Benjamin Bing told someone."

"In other words, what you're saying then is that without realising it, she must've been bang on target with her suspi-cions," said David. Then, when Mrs. Charles nodded, "I'll have to tell Merton about this, you know." He grinned a little. "It's going to wipe the smile off his face about you and the Laffont ladies, I can tell you."

Mrs. Charles did not respond. There was a faraway look in her eye. Then, after a few moments, she said, "If Tony was on her way to Glasgow the night she died, who or what was she going up there to see?" she paused for a moment. "Mrs. Flegg spoke of an elderly man—an American tourist—who stumbled across Dr. MacDonald's body in the graveyard. But he surely would've returned home by now. The doctor died some months before Tony made the connection with his murder and what happened to the judge."

"Maybe she made inquiries and found out that he was still around. I'll see what I can find out—what his name is and where he was staying when he made his statement to the police up there."

Mrs. Charles looked at him. "That's odd, Superintendent. It's just occurred to me. An elderly man gave evidence at Tony's inquest—a Scot, I think. . . . Yes, I remember now. He was travelling on the same train, and he was the last person to see her alive. And here's another odd thing. One of the last people to see the judge alive was an elderly New

Zealand–born author who was doing some preliminary research for a book he proposed to write on Pym and his trial. He lunched with the judge the day the judge died.

"Three elderly gentlemen, all with very distinct accents—one American, one Scot, and one New Zealander." The clairvoyante's eyes widened interrogatively. "Another of those curious coincidences you warned me not to read too much into, Superintendent?"

CHAPTER THIRTEEN

Mrs. Charles was thinking about her brother, wondering whether he had remembered to eat anything that day and whether she should make him a ham salad and take it down the road, when the telephone rang. It was David Sayer and he sounded agitated.

"We're in trouble, Madame," he began. "That conversation we had this morning about taking Merton into our confidence . . . Well, I don't mind telling you, right now I know just how Daniel must've felt. I've literally stepped into the lion's den and out again. I'm unscathed for the moment, but it isn't going to last, make no mistake about it. Merton's up to his neck in a murder investigation. Roger Purdie—*the* Roger Purdie . . . the publican who perjured himself at Pym's trial—was killed late last night, murdered out the back of his premises soon after closing time, the police think. His body wasn't discovered until this morning. His daughter found him out by the dustbins."

David paused. Then, "I don't like to complain, Madame—and I know I've said this to you before—but you don't half get me into some dodgy situations."

"Have you spoken personally to Merton?" she asked.

"Now isn't the time, Madame. Take my word for it. You haven't heard the rest of it yet. Remember that warning you gave me about Fullbright? Well, it seems you were a little late. Fullbright and Purdie were attacked one after the other. . . . Fullbright first—on a stretch of common ground across the way from Purdie's pub. An elderly jogger spotted Fullbright and the dog laid out amongst some bushes around 6 A.M. this morning. . . . Some old boy who claims he regu-

larly jogs through that patch. He took a quick look at Fullbright, thought he was drunk, then took another look and
jogged straight on to the police station to report what he'd
seen."

"Fullbright's dead?"

"Not so far as I know. He was only badly concussed. But
his dog was a goner. Anyway, Merton's got his hands full at
the moment. He's not going to want to hear me waffling on
about your suspicions over Tony Manners, etcetera. This is
all off the record, by the way, but he's got a suspect for
Purdie's murder and the attempt on Fullbright's life. . . . A
kid by the name of Flegg. Another good reason, I thought,
for giving Merton a wide berth for the present. That's if this
young man and Dr. MacDonald's former housekeeper are in
any way related."

There was a small pause. Then Mrs. Charles asked, "Was
there a robbery at The Ugly Duckling last night?"

"Not that I know of. Why?"

"I was just curious, that's all, Superintendent," she replied. "How serious do you think things are for the young
man?"

"Fairly serious, I'd say. There are witnesses—including
Purdie's daughter—to an argument Purdie had soon after
closing time with young Flegg and a few of his mates. Afterwards, Flegg split up with his mates and went back to the
pub and finished Purdie off. Independent witnesses have
said all the boys were drunk. And Flegg was seen crossing
alone to the common where he apparently relieved poor old
Fullbright of the cash in his wallet—clubbed him about the
head with the leg of some old furniture he'd found lying
somewhere about the place and bashed in the dog's head—
and then turned back to the pub after Purdie."

"How was Purdie killed?"

"With the same chunk of wood. You could see the dog
hairs sticking to it. That's how they know that the attack on
Purdie took place after Fullbright and his dog were set

upon." David hesitated. Then, "Well, Madame, now what are we going to do?"

The clairvoyante was quiet for a minute. Then she asked, "Where's Fullbright now?"

"In the special geriatric unit at Gidding General. He'll be kept there for a few days under observation. He's no spring chicken, you know. And he was lying unconscious throughout most of the night in all that rain."

"I think we should pay him a little visit, then, and cheer him up. What about tomorrow afternoon—if you're not busy, that is?"

"God help us if Merton finds out we're meddling in this," David warned her.

"Oh, I think we can safely rely on someone to tell him," said the clairvoyante with a small smile. "There's not much that I do that Mr. Merton doesn't eventually get to hear about."

"Yes," said David. "That's what I'm afraid of."

They found Martin Fullbright tucked up in a dark plaid blanket in an old bath chair out on a wide verandah sunning himself. A small transistor radio peeped over the top of the breast pocket of his maroon, black, and white Paisley dressing gown.

Fullbright apologised for not rising to greet his visitors, who, at his invitation, seated themselves in pink-painted wicker chairs at either side of him.

Mrs. Charles recognised him instantly. He was the partially sighted old man who had been pottering about in the grounds of the Brayside Infants School. She was not sure if he remembered speaking to her. He certainly made no sign to this effect.

The first thing which struck Mrs. Charles about his appearance in these more intimate circumstances was the aptness of Rendell Pym's alleged description of him, how very apelike the ex-detective chief superintendent of police was. Fullbright's coarse, bristly grey hair (and he had a lot of it, frizzing grotesquely at the open neck of his boldly striped pyjama jacket and covering his forearms where his sleeves had ridden up) would once have been very dark, almost black, she imagined. His enormous false teeth reminded her of those of the wolf dressed up as grandmother in "Little Red Riding Hood." (All the better to eat you with, my dear! she thought with a small shudder as he pulled back his unshaven top lip in what she assumed was meant to be a welcoming smile.)

David introduced himself and reminded Fullbright of their meeting at the time of the Pym murder investigation, at the mention of which Fullbright waved a dismissive hand in the air and nodded. Then David introduced Mrs. Charles, who was, he explained, carrying out some private inquiries on behalf of a client into the death of a young former W.P.C. whom Fullbright, he expected, would again remember from the time of the Pym investigation, Antonia Manners.

"Manners?" said Fullbright vaguely. "Oh, yes . . . I remember. Too soft for police work. Would've been better off as a social worker. Dead, is she?"

"Tony committed suicide two months ago," replied Mrs. Charles.

"Fancy," said Fullbright. He could not have made his total indifference to this piece of news plainer. Nor the fact that he had not much liked the girl. He dismissed her both from his mind and the conversation by gingerly fingering the lower part of his face and apologising for not having shaved that day. "Skin's still sensitive from the sticking plaster that young scum who attacked me stuck all over my mouth," he explained.

Mrs. Charles and David exchanged quick glances, but before either one of them could say anything, Fullbright went on.

"My own fault. I should've had more sense and listened to Blackie and stayed in. My dog," he added. "He knew something was wrong. First time I can remember him not wanting to go out for a walk. All on edge he was. Getting cranky in his old age, I thought." Fullbright waved an arm about in the air. "Anyway, they've caught up with the blighter—Flegg. Heard it on the wireless just a few minutes ago. Town's full of his type these days. Not safe for anybody to step outside their front door, day or night. Worse for us old folk. We're easy prey."

"That's the only explanation you can come up with for the attack on you, Mr. Fullbright?" asked the clairvoyante, eyeing the wide strip of surgical dressing on the left side of his forehead.

"What other explanation could there be?" he rejoined.

"You never, for example, associated the attack on you with your involvement in the Pym murder investigation some years ago?"

Mrs. Charles ignored the startled expression on David's face at the directness of her question and concentrated solely on the reaction of the man to whom she was speaking.

Slowly, Fullbright turned his partially sighted eyes full on her, and then, in a faintly irritated gesture, he put a hand to his head and jiggled the dark sunglasses he was wearing. Mrs. Charles could not see his eyes, but she could feel the contempt both they and the man's deliberately prolonged silence held for her.

"Pym?" As Fullbright said the name his mouth soured. "You're not suggesting that Flegg is in some way connected with that villain?"

"Is he, Mr. Fullbright?" she asked quietly.

A frown appeared on Fullbright's broad forehead. "In only one way as far as I'm concerned. They were both dirty cowards, killers of the worst kind and beneath contempt. Pym *savagely*"—Fullbright's face contorted in a fierce grimace—"murdering his sweet young wife, and now this other young villain committing a senselessly savage act against the father of his girlfriend. Miserable cowards, the pair of them. *Scum!*" Fullbright spat out the word with such vehemence that his false teeth shifted in his mouth, and he very nearly lost control of them.

Mrs. Charles studied his dark glasses for a moment before asking, "Did you actually see this young man attack you?"

Again the clairvoyante felt the full weight of the ex-police officer's contempt as he turned his gaze upon her. He gave her an unpleasant smile. "I've heard of you, Madame. Making quite a name for yourself . . . Things have certainly changed since my day. No amateurs, gifted or otherwise, would've got a look in . . . not on any case of mine, they wouldn't."

David was about to come to the clairvoyante's defence, but she silenced him with a quick warning glance. Then she said, "I'm flattered that you've heard of me, Mr. Fullbright."

He looked at her steadily. "It's a sewer out there." He waved one of his hairy arms in the air. "A sewer full of rats like Pym and Flegg who don't care"—he snapped his fingers —"for human life once they're cornered and their own precious necks are at stake. Tell me, Madame, I'd dearly love to know, how you'd go about tackling vermin like that once you'd cornered them."

"I think you've misunderstood the true nature of the role I play."

Fullbright was nodding his head. "One of those, eh? The armchair psychologists' brigade . . . *I understand, Mr. Pym,*" he said mincingly. *"You must trust me, Mr. Pym. Come and sit on my lap, Mr. Pym, and tell the nice lady all about your horrid childhood . . . how nobody understood you and your old man got drunk every Saturday night and thrashed the living daylights out of you, and your mother ran around with other men and never really cared what happened to you. . . ."*

He dropped the affected manner of speech.

"My God, it makes me sick! All this namby-pambying of criminals that goes on today."

Mrs. Charles said, "Did you always feel so strongly about the criminals with whom you came in contact?"

"As I did about Pym, you mean?"

"Yes."

Fullbright was quiet for a moment, considering the question. "No," he said at length. "Pym was special."

"Why? Because the Appeal Court quashed his sentence?"

Fullbright did not answer immediately. Then, in a very slow and deliberate voice, he said, "Rendell Pym was guilty of that murder, Madame. As true as you see me sitting here today, he savagely beat his wife to death, and then he spat contemptuously in everyone's eye."

A strange, faraway look crossed the old man's face. He spoke distantly. "A callous, cold-blooded murderer, the judge called him. Got that bit right. Went clean off the rails in his summing up, though. Unpremeditated, he said it was —the murder of Mrs. Pym." Fullbright was laughing softly and shaking his head. "No, Madame. Pym planned that murder right down to the very last detail after he'd discovered that his wife was unfaithful and was planning to leave him for her current lover, a chap by the name of Krendel."

Mrs. Charles said inquiringly, "The man Pym himself claimed killed his wife and who later admitted to having removed a diary of names from the floor beside Mrs. Pym's body?"

"I know very little about that, Madame. The matter was by then out of my hands. I was no longer stationed at Lymstead when that particular piece of evidence was turned up." Fullbright hesitated. "I was transferred to a place called Uppingham soon after Pym's trial. There was a nasty bit of business I looked into there before I retired from the force. . . ."

David caught Mrs. Charles's eye and gave her a meaningful look. She looked back at Fullbright when he said, "But I heard about it, of course. That Krendel eventually admitted taking a diary from the scene of the crime."

"And?" said Mrs. Charles when he paused.

"I'm sorry," he said. "I don't think I understand what you mean."

"You must have felt something—had some thoughts about this fresh evidence?"

"Yes," he admitted after another small pause. "I felt it was all a little too convenient. I have never, not for one moment, doubted that I arrested the right man for the murder of Pamela Pym." He pulled back his top lip in a sneering smile. "Before I'd finished with Pym, I'd crawled inside his head and taken a good look round. I knew how his brain worked. Cunning, he was, one of the most artfully sly villains I ever came up against."

He suddenly gave himself a little shake and looked quickly about him. "I wonder what time it is? Must be nearly tea-time. All this talking has made me hungry."

Abruptly he turned to David. "I don't suppose you've heard when I'll be able to return to work?"

"You have a job, Mr. Fullbright?" inquired the clairvoyante.

"At my age and half blind with it, you mean?" he said. "I'm not quite ready for the knackers' yard yet, Madame."

"I'm sorry if I've offended you. That was not my intention," she said. "If I seemed surprised, it was merely an expression of my admiration in the light of your physical disability."

He waved her apology aside. "Take no notice of me, Madame. My bark's a lot worse than my bite, I assure you." He fixed her with another of his alarming smiles. "Nice little job I've got. Not too physically or mentally taxing. Really, all I've got to do is to live on the premises and see to it that no one breaks in after school's out and vandalizes the building. Interesting sort of school. At least, you'd think so. Proper little bunch of terrorists, as far as I'm concerned. Caught a couple of them once out in the garden shed making a bomb. *A bomb*, if you please! A pair of eight-year-olds! More chance of them blowing themselves up than anyone else. Just got there in the nick of time."

"How long have you been there?" Mrs. Charles hesitated. "I assume you're talking about the Brayside Infants School."

He nodded. "Ever since I retired. Just over ten years. It wasn't always a school. It used to be a private nursing home.

I lived there with my sister until the place was closed down, then I stayed on as caretaker—my sister emigrated to Australia. My sister's daughter and her family were already out there, and I intended to join them. But then, time went by, the home was sold, and then I was asked by the new owner, the principal of the infants school, if I'd stay on in Rosa's old flat and continue to keep an eye on the place. So I never got to go to Australia," he grinned. "But who knows, one of these days I might make it out there . . . give Rosa a surprise."

"You're Rosa Trumble's brother?" Mrs. Charles was momentarily nonplussed. Then, still very puzzled, "But Mr. Fullbright, from the way you've been speaking about Rendell Pym, I naturally assumed that you and he . . . that your paths never crossed again."

"They didn't," he said.

Mrs. Charles looked at him, frowned. "But Mr. Fullbright, I understand that it was to Mrs. Rosa Trumble's—*your sister's*—nursing home, The Grange, that Pym was sent after his nervous breakdown."

"Two different people," said Fullbright.

CHAPTER FOURTEEN

Mrs. Charles looked blankly at David, then back again at Martin Fullbright.

"You're asking me to believe that there were *two* Rendell Pyms? The one you knew and the one who later came into your sister's care?"

"Yes, Madame. Pym *was* two different people. I think you might've misunderstood me. The only thing the two men had in common was the past, the crime for which Pym had been tried. But as for their personalities, even their physical appearance, they were as different as chalk is to cheese. The Pym I'd known was a mean, callous, cruel, vicious, foul-mouthed killer—a hulking great *brute* of a man in every sense of the word. But the nervous breakdown—"

Fullbright paused and shook his head. "I'd never have thought something like that could so change a man. Pym didn't exactly go round quoting passages from the Bible, but if he had, I, for one, wouldn't have been at all surprised. I was suspicious to begin with. All a big act, I thought. . . . The man was a gifted actor, you know. Put on all the Christmas shows at The Grange, and one year, I remember, he did a takeoff of Rosa. Borrowed some of her clothes—one of her uniforms and a white veil and her starched apron and all that—brought the house down! I tell you that man could impersonate anybody . . . the way they walked, the way they talked." Fullbright was shaking his head wonderingly. "Rosa was my sister, but I wouldn't have been able to tell the difference between them, not from where I was sitting, anyway. It was a brilliant impersonation. Rosa was a big woman with plenty of flesh on her bones—whereas the breakdown had turned Pym into a walking skeleton."

Fullbright frowned reflectively. "Never knew how he achieved that—Rosa's full cheeks. But I daresay he just padded his out with something. D'you know that man's hair fell out? Had a head of hair like mine—thicker, in fact—and yet it all dropped out, every single strand of it! Later some grew down each side and round the back, but he never had a full head of hair again. That's the only thing I've ever been afraid of," confessed the old man with a shudder. "Going bald. *Nasty!*"

He thought about it for a moment. Then, shaking his head again, "No, the only thing that I could see that definitely hadn't changed about Pym was his attitude to dogs. He couldn't stand them, and they couldn't stand him. Can't say I've ever cared all that much for them myself. That was the one thing we had in common—and the only thing, I might add! Even Blackie—my sister's dog—was anathema to him. And Pym was fond of Rosa . . . well, I say *fond*, but I guess I really mean totally dependent on her. Rosa saved his life, there's no doubt about that, just like there's no doubt that it was Rosa's dog who saved my life the other night. Rosa couldn't take poor old Blackie with her when she went out to Australia—the strict quarantine regulations—so he stayed behind to keep me company.

"But as I was saying about Pym, he was sent to Rosa to die —there's no doubt about that. But Rosa wasn't having any of that nonsense. Remarkable gift that woman has for healing, and not just the body, the mind as well. Until I saw what happened to him (and I don't mind telling you that I was *incensed* when Rosa told me who her latest patient was), I would never have believed that the state of one's mind could so destroy an individual physically. Rosa made me go with her to Pym's room and take a good long look at him. He was so weak he couldn't walk, couldn't even lift an arm to feed himself. 'And you hate *that* pathetic creature?' Rosa said to me. 'Can't you see,' she said, 'that whatever sins that man has committed he's paying for far more cruelly and harshly this way than he ever would've done under any punishment the courts might've meted out to him?'

"And it was true." Fullbright nodded. "If it came down to a choice, I reckon I would've preferred the gallows to what Pym suffered. He went through a complete metamorphosis. The man who went into a nervous breakdown, and became cocooned in it, emerged as an entirely different person. All he wanted was to be left in peace with his garden, to be allowed to organise the Christmas party, and to be near Rosa. I don't mean that he was in love with her. I don't think either Pym—the one I knew or the man he became under Rosa's influence—was capable of love or affection. Not made that way myself, so I understood the man there, just as I understood his need for Rosa, his dependence on her. She kept him alive. She was his strength. And that was what killed him . . . when they decided to close the home and Rosa told him she was leaving the country for good."

"How did Pym die, Mr. Fullbright?" asked the clairvoyante.

"He killed himself. The very day Rosa left. He went missing. . . . There were still several patients waiting to be found somewhere to go—the difficult ones to relocate . . . people like Pym, who weren't really sick as such but who were no longer capable of living on the outside—and a few of us went looking for him. It took us a while, but we eventually found him over by the railway line about a quarter of a mile away. He'd jumped from a footbridge into the path of an oncoming train."

"How very sad," murmured Mrs. Charles softly.

Fullbright made no comment. There was a small, thoughtful pause. Then Mrs. Charles went on.

"I don't suppose there could be any mistake about it. . . . It was Rendell Pym you found by the railway line?"

"The man was a mess right enough," said Fullbright bluntly. "But it was Pym all right. Nobody could put anything like that over me—though I admit that the Pym of old

I'd known and despised would've tried. Right up his street that would've been, trying to put one over on me." He grinned unpleasantly. "No, Madame. This old police dog wasn't born yesterday. It was Rendell Maxwell Pym, wife murderer, who was picked up off that railway line that day. You can take my word for it!"

Mrs. Charles and David walked slowly down the wide hospital corridor towards the exit.

"Fullbright'll go for that lad the same way he did for Pym," remarked David. "Did you notice? He never answered when you asked if he saw who attacked him. He's no more idea who struck him and the dog down than I have. But for reasons best known to Fullbright himself, Flegg—like Pym before him—fits his bill, and so he'll make sure he gets him. Oh, and by the way! That move he spoke of to Uppingham . . . He was transferred there deliberately soon after Pym's trial. It was the first step towards easing him permanently out of the force."

They passed through the glass swing-doors and walked towards the car park.

"Er, I hope you won't take this the wrong way and think I'm abandoning you in your hour of need, Madame, but I don't honestly think it would be a terribly good idea to raise the matter of Tony Manners's death with Merton. I admit you've turned up some pretty strange coincidences, but . . ."

She looked at him thoughtfully when he paused. "You still think I could be reading too much into them?"

"It's one of the risks you take when you start analysing a coincidence too closely, the danger that you'll pick and pull at it until you shape it the way you'd like to see it. Lymstead is a very small place, Madame. I'm sorry, but I could quite readily accept that young Flegg—the son of the housekeeper of one of the chief prosecution witnesses at Pym's trial—could unknowingly mug an old man who happened to have been another witness at that same trial and also have a personal problem with a further witness, Purdie, which unfortunately resolved itself in murder. An odd coincidence, admittedly, but coincidence all the same. In a small place like Lymstead, people's paths are almost certainly going to cross at some point."

Mrs. Charles smiled faintly at him. "I'm not sure if it's me you're trying to convince or yourself, Superintendent."

He wagged his head at her. "You're going to come a cropper on this one, Madame. Don't give Merton that satisfaction."

"You honestly think it's mere coincidence that three prominent figures at the trial of Rendell Pym should in the first instance have his eyes taped over, in the second have his one good ear taped up, and in the third have his mouth taped shut?"

"Madame," said David, "it is not uncommon for victims of a vicious physical attack to be left in the way that MacDonald and Fullbright were so that (a) in MacDonald's case, the attacker cannot be identified, and (b) the victim cannot cry out. As for Halahan—well, let's face it. The old boy was probably gaga. Had to be. Lying there dying in his butler's arms and all the silly old beggar can think of to say is to tell his faith healer that the pain has come back."

He shook his head at the sudden look the clairvoyante shot at him. "I'm sorry to be so callous, Madame. But really—a headache should've been the least of his worries. In the circumstances."

Mrs. Charles eyed him speculatively. "But what if Ramsay misheard him?" she said.

"How do you mean?"

She was quiet for a moment. Then, pensively, "What if Halahan said *Pym?* 'Tell Bing. *Pym* is back.' "

David stared at her. "You're obsessed, you know that, don't you?"

"As well as being right, I hope, Superintendent." She hesitated. Then, in a distant voice, "You know what that would mean, don't you? Pym has to be alive."

David shook his head. "No, Madame. Pym is dead."

"Then somebody is impersonating him."

"How do you make that out?"

"Quite easily. The facts speak for themselves. The impersonator was careless. One of his victims—the judge—saw his face and lived long enough to identify him."

CHAPTER FIFTEEN

Neville Krendel was serving a customer when Mrs. Charles entered his shop early the next day. A pregnant young woman in a short smock and black slacks sat on a stool behind the counter languidly smoking a cigarette. She looked bored and did not appear to notice, or possibly even care, that another customer was perhaps requiring some assistance.

At length the young woman looked disinterestedly round at Mrs. Charles and said, in a flat voice, "Oh. Yes? Were you wanting something?"

"Good morning. Are you Mrs. Krendel?" inquired the clairvoyante.

The young woman nodded and said she was.

"I wonder if I might have a word with Mr. Krendel, please?" said Mrs. Charles.

"He's busy at the moment," replied Mrs. Krendel.

"I can wait," said the clairvoyante.

Mrs. Krendel averted her face and lapsed back into her reverie. Mrs. Charles could see only a slight resemblance in her to her mother, Dolly Dackers, mostly about the eyes, which had an almost Oriental slant to them. Mrs. Charles continued to watch the side of her face for a moment. The young woman's lack of mobility and vitality went far beyond the limitations placed on her by her present physical condition and was as inherent in her as the extreme opposite was true of her mother, thought the clairvoyante. Where the older woman bubbled and effervesced, the flame in the younger one had not yet even begun to be kindled.

Finally, the other customer departed, and Neville

Krendel, without looking Mrs. Charles's way, moved to the rear of the shop and began to vacuum up seed husks from a parrot's cage. His wife made no attempt to draw his attention to the fact that there was someone waiting to speak to him.   —

Mrs. Charles hesitated momentarily and then walked down to him. She had to raise her voice over the din the vacuum cleaner was making in order to be heard.

"Mr. Krendel?"

He was smoking a pipe, which he grasped firmly between his large, nicotine-stained teeth before nodding. He did not turn off the cleaner. His grizzled hair reached down to his shoulders, although he was quite bald on top of his head, and he wore a long, old-fashioned bushy beard. His manner, as Mrs. Flegg had more or less intimated, was casual to the point of insolence.

"I wonder if I might have a word with you, please? In private," added the clairvoyante as the door to the street opened and a man came into the shop.

The racket of the vacuum cleaner began to get on the parrot's nerves, and it screeched protestingly and climbed the sides of its cage.

Without removing the pipe from his mouth, Neville Krendel jerked his head at the young woman sitting on the stool at the other end of the shop and said, "If you wouldn't mind . . . My wife will help you."

"I doubt it," said Mrs. Charles. "Mrs. Krendel couldn't have been much more than five or six years old when Pamela Pym was murdered."

Krendel looked hard at her, then bit on the stem of his pipe and went on vacuuming up the seed husks. The other customer, having abandoned all hope of being served by Mrs. Krendel, had moved further down the shop and hovered uncertainly behind Mrs. Charles. Krendel ignored him. To the parrot, he said coldly, "I think you'd better leave, and I'll thank you never to come in my shop again."

The man hovering nearby gave him a startled look, hesitated doubtfully, and then, as casually as he could, turned and drifted slowly out of the shop. Through a haze of cigarette smoke, Mrs. Krendel watched him leave, then stirred from the stool. Leaning forward over the counter, she called down the shop to her husband, "Coffee?"

Krendel's emotionless grey eyes met Mrs. Charles's unwavering gaze, then he stooped to switch off the cleaner. When he rose, Mrs. Charles had turned her back on him and was walking away.

"Who was that?" asked his wife, waddling up to him.

"Just somebody wanting to put up a notice about something or other in the window. I told her we don't do that sort of thing."

"Oh," said his wife. She stretched up her arms and yawned. Then, after a moment, "I'll go up and get the coffee. Won't be long."

She disappeared through a side door to their flat.

Her husband listened to her slow, heavy tread on the stairs. Then, when he heard her footsteps echoing directly overhead, he went quickly to the telephone and dialled a number.

"Dolly?" he said after a few moments. "Neville. I've just had a visitor. . . ."

Upstairs in the flat, Tina Krendel bit her bottom lip and carefully picked up the receiver on the extension line, held it to her ear. She heard her mother's voice.

"Damn! What did she want?"

"I didn't ask."

"You're sure it was the same woman who was snooping at the meeting the other night?"

"Tall, blond, mid to late forties, talking about the Pyms. How much closer do you need to get?" he snapped.

"All right—don't get shirty!" The woman at the end of the line paused. Then, "It was a lucky thing you couldn't be there on Tuesday night."

"Wasn't it just?" he said sarcastically. "How the hell did she get onto me, that's what I'd like to know?"

"Why don't you tell him, Mum?" Tina Krendel's voice suddenly cut in. "Tell him what you told me . . . about how you were so jealous of us you told lies about him to that private investigator about all the birds that have been stolen lately. Just like you told lies about him when Mrs. Pym was killed."

There was a deathly silence. Then Krendel finally took the pipe from his mouth and said, "What's all this then, Dolly?"

"That woman at the meeting on Tuesday night—the one who was just in the shop," said Tina Krendel when her mother failed to reply. "Mum told me she was also asking questions about Tony Manners."

Mrs. Dackers slowly put down the telephone receiver and gazed bleakly at the bare wall before her. How was she supposed to know that that girl had been involved with the Pyms. It was Neville who used to loaf about the house all day looking after Tina and watching the neighbours' comings and goings, she thought bitterly. And anyway, it was all his fault. None of this would've happened if he hadn't treated her so shabbily. He had no one but himself to blame. . . .

Mrs. Charles knocked on the door of flat number 8 and waited. The caretaker had told her that Mrs. Flegg was in, she hadn't gone out to work at all so far that morning.

"The poor woman has hardly set foot outside her front door since they came and told her the bad news about that lad of hers," he had added, shaking his head pityingly.

After a very long wait, the door of the flat finally opened a crack and a dull voice said, "Yes, who is it?"

"It's Edwina Charles, Mrs. Flegg," replied the clairvoyante.

There was a small pause, and then Mrs. Flegg said, "I'm sorry, I don't mean to be rude, but I'm not feeling very well this morning. Could you come back some other time?"

There was another small pause. Then Mrs. Charles said, "I

was very sorry to hear about your son's trouble, Mrs. Flegg. I'd like to help if I can."

"That's very kind of you, thank you, but no one can do anything now, it's too late."

"It will be if you don't make some positive effort of your own about his predicament," said the clairvoyante quietly. "Your son is in very serious trouble, and from my understanding of his situation, I'm not at all sure that the kind of justice he'll get won't be the rough sort if he isn't helped and helped quickly."

There was a slight hesitation, then Mrs. Flegg said dispiritedly, "It's all very well for you to talk like that, but what can I do?"

"You could start by asking me in and talking to me."

The door opened and Mrs. Flegg looked at her. Her eyes were bewildered, red-rimmed with crying. "I don't understand any of this," she said after a moment.

"No, neither do I," said the clairvoyante. "What the police allege your son did to Mr. Purdie would only make sense to me if The Ugly Duckling had also been robbed, which it wasn't."

Mrs. Flegg stared at her for a second or two, then stood aside to let her in.

"Nobody said anything to me about that sort of robbery," said Mrs. Flegg as she closed the door.

"No, and for the simple reason that there wasn't one," said Mrs. Charles, turning to face her. "And as far as I'm concerned, the two would've gone hand in hand if it were your son who attacked Mr. Purdie. Believe me, Mrs. Flegg," the clairvoyante went on quietly. "I know. . . ."

Mrs. Flegg looked at her despairingly. "But Trev had Mr. Purdie's blood all over his clothes. His fingerprints were on the piece of wood the police say Mr. Purdie was killed with." She hesitated, frowned at the thoughtful look on Mrs. Charles's face. "You didn't know that, did you?" she said slowly.

"No," Mrs. Charles admitted. Then, after a pause, "Where was your son picked up by the police?"

"Here. He was still in bed when they came round and took him away for questioning."

"Have you spoken to him since?"

Mrs. Flegg bowed her head, gave it a slight shake. "I went down to the police station, but he won't say anything to anybody. He's even refusing to be represented by a solicitor. They haven't arrested him yet—charged him with murder. I understand there's a possibility that he could be appearing briefly in court later this morning while the police apply to have him remanded in custody for a few days while they complete their inquiries. I'm not really sure what's going on. . . ." Tears began to roll slowly down her pale cheeks. "It's all so confusing. Nobody will tell me anything. If only he'd be sensible and cooperate. He's only making things worse for himself by refusing to speak."

"What time did he come home on Tuesday night?" asked Mrs. Charles.

Mrs. Flegg dried her eyes and blew her nose. Then, shaking her head, she took a deep breath and said, "I'm not sure, I didn't look at the time. About eleven, I think. He was in one of his bad moods again—I could tell that by the way he slammed the front door when he came in and then shuffled his feet. He always drags his feet when he's sulking about something. So I left him right alone. We only end up having words if I try and talk to him when he's like that. He went straight to his room—slammed that door too. So, like I said, I left him to it. The next thing I knew, the police were hammering on the door looking for him."

Mrs. Flegg wiped a hand tiredly across her eyes. "He's just like his father. I could never get him to talk about things either. That's why our marriage broke up. He just used to sit and brood and think everyone was against him. I could never get him to see that the only person who was ever really against him was himself. And Trev's just the same . . . thinks the whole wide world owes him a living, and then when it doesn't give him what he wants just when he wants it, he blames everybody but himself. He's had five jobs since he left school, and the longest he's lasted in any of them was one week. My sister Liz says it's all my fault, I've been too soft with him, spoilt him. But I can't see that I have. The Good Lord knows I've done everything I can to give him a decent upbringing. I've tried my best to teach him right from wrong. But you can't go against the genes, can you? Trev's trouble is the same as his father's. There's no reasoning with them. They both think they're so much cleverer than anyone else," she finished with a trace of bitterness.

"Has Trevor ever physically harmed anyone before, Mrs. Flegg?" asked Mrs. Charles.

"Never." Mrs. Flegg shook her head emphatically. "He's been in trouble with the police, though. But not for anything serious." Mrs. Flegg frowned quickly. "He's never had to appear in court or anything like that. Trev's never been violent. He doesn't even get cheeky with people. He's more the moody type, like I said. He just sits about and sulks when he can't get his own way, or if he thinks he's been done down. He's always been like it, even as a little boy. It's never been in his nature to fight back. He just comes home and goes all quiet." Mrs. Flegg paused. Then, anxiously, "If only I knew what was going on . . . I feel sick with worry."

Mrs. Charles opened her handbag and took out a small white business card. Handing it to Mrs. Flegg, she said, "I would like you to promise me you'll phone me any time, day or night, if you feel you need someone to talk to. In the meanwhile, I'll see what I can find out for you, though I can't promise anything. I have a friend who might be able to help."

She saw the puzzled look on Mrs. Flegg's face as she read the name on the card.

"Adele Herrmann is the name I use professionally," explained Mrs. Charles. "Herrmann is my maiden name."

Mrs. Flegg looked up slowly at her.

"You're not a private investigator?" She looked back at the card. "You're a . . . *clairvoyante?*"

"I used to think so," replied Mrs. Charles with a wry smile.

CHAPTER SIXTEEN

Ernest Hammond's young trainee negotiator looked up quickly from his desk as the door to the street opened, his expression changing to one of hopeful anticipation as he recognised the woman who came in. Without her weedy brother, the young man noted with some relief. We've struck oil here, my old son, he said to himself as he got up and approached the counter with a welcoming smile.

"Good morning," he said. "Mrs. Charles, isn't it? You've made up your mind, have you?"

The clairvoyante returned his smile. "There are just one or two matters I'd like to raise with Mr. Hammond," she said. "That's if he's in at the moment."

So great was the young man's delight at having (or so he assumed) successfully negotiated the reletting of "the dump round the corner," as the staff of Hammond & Co. were in the habit of referring to the vacant office accommodation over the dry cleaner's in Mallard Lane, that he almost blurted out, "Yes, Mr. Hammond's out the back counting his money." (A literal truth. Ernest Hammond personally collected the rents in cash of some of his properties, those in the poorer parts of town.) Instead, the young man said, "I'll see if he's free. I won't keep you a moment."

Had it been any property other than the one his young negotiator assured him his prospective client was "dead keen on," Ernest Hammond would have insisted that he could not be disturbed. Counting his money was one of the few treats he permitted himself. In fact, his only treat. Visiting Alice Laffont once every eight days (as prescribed by some old sage in an ancient sex manual his father had pressed on him shortly before young Ernest had embarked upon holy matrimony) was more of a medicinal nature. He went there these days purely for health reasons, which justified the extravagance. But only just.

Mrs. Charles was obliged to wait almost ten minutes while Mr. Hammond got his money safely tucked away out of sight. Then the beaming young negotiator was instructed to show his prospective client through.

The main outer office was modern and quite comfortably furnished. Mr. Hammond's own office was Spartan. One desk, the chair in which he sat, a typist's chair for the use of anyone who might wish to speak with him (the extreme uncomfortability of this particular chair ensuring that no one outstayed his welcome), and, close by, at his right hand, a small wooden cupboard, which Mrs. Charles guessed contained a safe. On top of the cupboard were some legal books and a local street directory. There was a small, insect-specked calendar on the wall, but it was two years out of date. There were no curtains on the window, which needed cleaning.

Ernest Hammond himself looked much as the clairvoyante remembered him from their one meeting fifteen years ago when she had bought The Bungalow. He half rose as she entered his office, and a small coin, which had dropped unnoticed from the desk onto his lap, rolled across the carpet and clinked against something. Recognising the sound, the estate agent looked quickly about the floor, trying to locate the vanished coin. Then, reluctantly abandoning the search for the present, he nodded at his prospective client and then indicated his shiny pink, balding head to the typist's chair. The liver-spotted, podgy hands which had gripped the arms of his chair and pushed him upwards remained there.

"Good morning," he said. His preoccupation with money only a few minutes before and the prospect now of acquiring some more had achieved a clarity of mind and purpose which the clairvoyante, recalling her previous encounter with him, could only hope would outlast her visit. He went straight on.

"I understand you're interested in the office accommodation we have available around the corner in Mallard Lane. Marvellous location. You couldn't wish for a more convenient spot. Post office not two minutes' walk away . . . all the major banks on hand. And, of course, the shops . . . Very important when it comes to recruiting staff, especially the married ladies. They do like to have their shops handy, don't they?"

"I'm sorry," said Mrs. Charles, stepping in quickly when he paused for breath. "There appears to have been some mistake. Your negotiator must have misunderstood. I really wanted to speak to you about the previous tenant of that property, Miss Antonia Manners."

Mr. Hammond's head drooped forward a little, and he fixed his large, prominent blue eyes on her. "What did you say your name was?" His tone of voice was both suspicious and challenging.

"Charles, Mrs. Edwina Charles," she replied, thoughtfully eyeing the chair which had been offered to her and then cautiously trying to locate its centre of gravity as her weight settled down on it.

"Oh," he said. Then, with an abrupt nod, "Yes, Mrs. Charles. Mimi Laffont and her sister, Alice, mentioned you." He paused, regarded her speculatively. "A lady private investigator, eh? Gidding seems to be overrun with them. Well," he went on in a grumbling voice. "What can I do for you?"

"The file Mrs. Laffont took from Tony's flat and destroyed—"

"Very foolish of her," Mr. Hammond interrupted. "I told her so too."

"You suspected that this file might've had some bearing on Tony's death?"

"What?" He looked startled. "No, of course not. The woman committed suicide. No doubt about it. The fact remains, though, that everything in her flat should've been left exactly as it was until the police had been round. In case there were problems with any of the relatives."

"Nevertheless you yourself did not hesitate to remove certain items from the flat," Mrs. Charles pointed out.

His eyes narrowed. "All my own property, Madame. And I never touched anything I couldn't rightly claim was mine. I might also add that I removed those items for the same reason that I felt Mimi and Alice should have left that file exactly where it was—to avoid complications with any of Miss Manners's relatives. I'd lost enough money over that young woman's tenancy without incurring the added expense of fighting her family in a court of law for what was legally mine."

"As you were obviously aware that there was a typewriter in the flat, you must have also known that Tony brought work home from the office. Does this mean you were familiar with the contents of the file and knew the nature of the case she was working on?"

"Absolutely not," he said. "I only knew about the typewriter because Alice told me it was there. And, of course, I knew immediately what Miss Manners's game was. She'd removed it from the office along with a number of other pieces of office equipment to prevent my seizing them in lieu of the rent she owed me. I was very grateful to Alice for keeping me informed of the situation. I can't tell you the amount of money I have to write off each year through bad tenants like Tony Manners.

"You were also Rendell Pym's landlord, weren't you?"

"Pym?" He stared at her. "What's he got to do with this?"

"Everything, Mr. Hammond. In my opinion, that is," said the clairvoyante. "I have good reason to believe that the file which Mimi Laffont destroyed contained information that Tony had gathered concerning certain persons involved in the police investigation into the murder of Pamela Pym and the subsequent trial of her husband for that crime."

The hands holding the arms of the chair tightened their grip perceptibly.

"That was all over and done with years ago," he said.

Mrs. Charles shook her head. She spoke slowly and deliberately. "I don't think so, Mr. Hammond. Are you aware, for instance, that two of the chief prosecution witnesses who were called to give evidence at Rendell Pym's trial and the judge—Mr. Justice Halahan—have all recently died in unusual circumstances, and that another witness only barely escaped with his life on Tuesday night after being savagely attacked while he was out walking with his dog?"

"I never gave evidence at the trial for or against Pym," he said defensively.

"No. I understand you didn't really come into things until Mrs. Finch—Mrs. Dackers as I believe she is now known, the Pyms' next-door neighbour—handed over Mrs. Pym's diary, which contained your name amongst others."

Ernest Hammond's head jutted forward. The pupils of his pale blue eyes were like fine black needle points. "Of course my name was in her diary. I was her landlord, wasn't I? My name was noted down on the day I collected the rent, once a week. Mrs. Pym had a shocking memory where money matters were concerned. She was very young, you know—half her husband's age—and Pym was away nine tenths of the time, so she had to make a note of things like that, otherwise she forgot all about them. I explained all this to the police." He frowned. "I really must say I object most strongly to being interrogated in this summary fashion. In fact, I shall seriously consider consulting my solicitor about this."

"Very wise," said Mrs. Charles.

He looked at her.

"I have already tentatively arranged for the whole matter to be placed before a senior member of the Gidding C.I.D.—Detective Chief Superintendent Clive Merton. Possibly you know him. . . . So I would think there are going to be quite a few more questions you're going to be asked, Mr. Hammond, before my inquiries into Tony Manners's death are complete."

He continued to look at her for another full minute. Then he cleared his throat. "Now look," he said. He smiled tremulously. "I mean, surely there's no need for that. I'm sorry if I got a bit high-handed, I forgot myself for a moment. You've got your job to do—I appreciate that. And I'm sure it can't be very nice for you . . . having to dig up all this unpleasantness. Look. If I tell you what you want to know, surely we can keep the matter from going any further than this room. I'll be blunt. I intend seeking reelection to Council. A scandal now—my name linked with a police inquiry"—his eyebrows rose—"or the Laffont sisters—do I make my meaning clear?—will not further my cause. If there are any questions to be answered—questions that I am able to answer, of course—then I would far rather that you should ask them now."

"Very well," said Mrs. Charles with a slow nod. "But actually there was only the one question I wanted to ask you, Mr. Hammond." She paused, watched his face closely. "Did you know about that file—the one Tony kept at the flat relating to certain parties who had been involved in the Pym murder investigation—prior to its being destroyed by Mimi Laffont?"

Ernest Hammond's gaze never wavered. "No," he said. "The first I knew of it was when Alice told me about it after I'd got round there that afternoon."

Mrs. Charles rose, only barely catching the chair she had been sitting on before it crashed to the floor. She paused and set it squarely on its splayed-out legs, then she said, "Thank you for your cooperation. Good day, Mr. Hammond."

He got up quickly and came round his desk and escorted her to the door.

"I had a client once by the name of Charles—sold her a nice little place over in Little Gidding. Gay divorcee. Pretty well-fixed financially, I heard. Stunning woman. Though no relation of yours, of course," he said.

Mrs. Charles looked into his eyes, but their expression was blandly innocent. If his parting remark had been a deliberate put-down, he was masking it well.

Bidding him a further good day, she walked out comforting herself with a highly unflattering picture of the tubby, money-hungry Ernest Hammond grubbing around on all fours on the floor of his office in search of the coin.

CHAPTER SEVENTEEN

It was raining when Mrs. Charles stepped down from the bus at four-fifteen that afternoon and made her way along the road to her home, and from the glistening dampness of the long grass growing along the verges and the number of muddy puddles lying about, it had been raining in that area for some while.

There was a shabby white van parked at a short distance from her bungalow. She glanced at it as she passed by. No one was in it, which rather made her think that it might have broken down and that the driver had walked back into the village for assistance.

Mrs. Charles was almost up to her front door before she heard someone call her name and turned to see Dolly Dackers, who had been sheltering from the rain behind a copper beech tree in the clairvoyante's front garden, hastening up the path towards her.

The tightly belted, beige trench coat Mrs. Dackers was wearing was very wet and gave the impression that she either had been caught in a heavy downpour or had been waiting about in the rain for quite some time.

As she came up to the clairvoyante, Mrs. Dackers said, "I'm sorry we didn't actually get round to speaking to one another the other night at the meeting. I had to leave early. . . ." She untied her wet headscarf and mopped her damp hair with it.

"Mrs. Dackers, isn't it?" said Mrs. Charles. "Mr. Ramsay mentioned your name."

"Such a nice, kind man," said the other woman, shaking out the scarf and then folding it into a neat square and pocketing it. "Our most successful medium. But I suppose you know all about that." The dazzling smile she turned on Mrs. Charles as she looked up from her pocket was brief. Abruptly inclining her head a little on one side, she frowned and said, "I know of your reputation, Madame. . . . You must be terribly busy, and I really ought to have phoned first for an appointment and not come straight on over here like this, but I simply had to see you."

"You'd better come in and get dry," said Mrs. Charles.

They went inside. Mrs. Charles took Mrs. Dackers's coat, then got her a towel and left her drying her face and hair in the sitting room while she made some tea.

"Now," she said when she rejoined her a short while later. "What was it you wanted to see me about so urgently?"

"I don't really know where to begin," said Mrs. Dackers. She looked at Mrs. Charles hesitantly, hoping she would say something, but the clairvoyante remained silent.

After a short wait, Mrs. Dackers went on reluctantly. "I know you must think this is none of my business, but Mr. Ramsay has been telling us—Mr. Bing and me—about the conversation you had with him about Rendell Pym the other night, and . . . well, I knew him—Rendell—knew him quite well, as a matter of fact." She tried to laugh off this statement lightly, but the sound she made was harsh and brittle. "Rendell and my late husband, Jack Dackers, were friends. I was only ever Finch's common-law wife—we never married, though I used his name for a time . . . until he walked out on me and went off with somebody else." Mrs. Dackers spoke as if it were an established fact between them that Mrs. Charles knew of this episode of her life. She went on.

"Anyway, as I said, Rendell and Jack were friends, and I wondered if I could help you." She smiled tentatively, fidgeted with the selvedge on the towel. "Not that I really know what it is you want to know. But like I said, I knew them—Rendell and Pam Pym. Certainly better than either Mr. Bing or Mr. Ramsay did. And poor Bing. He's such a

sensitive man." She laughed nervously. "These little things
do upset him so, I fear. He's led rather a sheltered life. Spent
too much time with his nose buried in fusty old law books."
She laughed again. "I don't really know what I'm going to do
about him—"

"You're here on his behalf?"

Mrs. Dackers gave another brittle little laugh. "Bing and I
are—well, what you might call courting. I try to smooth out
life's little humps and bumps for him. I'm sure you know
how it is."

Mrs. Charles looked at her. Then, after a moment or two,
"Did Mr. Bing tell you about the message he got through Mr.
Ramsay from Mr. Justice Halahan as the judge lay dying?"

"Oh, yes. . . . Poor soul. Bing was most distressed about
that. He was so sure he'd helped the dear old judge. And
dear Bing has so few failures. It undermines his confidence
so."

"But that wasn't what really upset him, was it, Mrs. Dackers?" Mrs. Charles spoke softly; she looked at the other
woman steadily. "Mr. Bing was upset because he knew the
judge's dying words were really a warning about Pym. . . .
That it was Rendell Pym, not the pain that was back."

Mrs. Dackers avoided looking at Mrs. Charles. She
reached for her tea.

"So you know about that," she said. Her voice had
changed completely. She was firmer, more resolute—and
somehow resigned, thought the clairvoyante.

Mrs. Dackers went on, "I knew the minute I found out
who you were that we were in trouble. I told Bing he was a
fool, he should've talked to you, told you the truth. Or at
least what he suspected was the truth. He can't help himself,
you know." She looked up at Mrs. Charles suddenly, her
finely plucked eyebrows arched. "He thinks twice and then
twice more before he'll say as much as good morning to the
milkman for fear he'll incriminate himself in some way. And
really, it wasn't until Tony Manners came to see him that the
penny dropped about Pym and the mistake John Ramsay

had made in thinking Mr. Halahan was talking about his migraine headaches."

"Did Tony tell Mr. Bing that she thought the judge had been murdered?"

"Absolute nonsense, of course." Mrs. Dackers laughed shortly and avoided looking at the other woman.

"Would you know if Tony mentioned Dr. MacDonald's death to Mr. Bing?" asked the clairvoyante.

Mrs. Dackers's head came up sharply, and she looked at her intently. Then she nodded. "Bing thought she was raving mad."

"But nevertheless her theory about the two deaths—the doctor's and the judge's—alarmed him?"

"Anything out of the ordinary, the slightest upset to his daily routine, and Bing panics. He can't help himself. He's led such a sheltered life, poor soul," said Mrs. Dackers dryly.

"Why should the judge feel the need to warn Mr. Bing specifically that Pym was back?"

Mrs. Dackers shook her head, frowned. "We don't know. Honestly we don't. I swear it! Bing never knew Pym. Not personally."

"But you did," said Mrs. Charles musingly. "Was the judge aware of your friendship with Mr. Bing?"

"Possibly." Mrs. Dackers hesitated. "He came along to a couple of our meetings. . . ." She hesitated again. "You don't think it was me he was really trying to warn? I mean— *why?* My affair with Rendell Pym was over a year or more before Rendell met and then married Pam. I can't say he and I finished up good friends, but we weren't exactly enemies either. I never did anything to hurt Rendell."

"Except alibi his wife's lover—the man Pym swore murdered his wife."

Mrs. Dackers's mouth set in a thin, straight line. "Rendell Pym killed his wife. Everybody knows that."

"And yet his appeal was upheld."

Mrs. Dackers laughed dryly. "Thanks to the mess that know-it-all copper made of the case. He should've left well enough alone. The truth would've come out eventually without anybody having to bend and twist the facts to fit. He pushed too hard, scared everybody off. People used to say that Rendell Pym was the man everybody loved to hate. . . . Well, let me tell you something—I've never disliked or feared anyone as much as I disliked and feared that copper. He terrified me. Even his sister, Rosa Trumble, didn't like him all that much. I didn't dare come forward and tell the truth until I found out he'd been transferred from Lymstead." She widened her eyes. "And don't think I don't know what you're thinking. Everybody thought the same thing. They said I did it out of spite. I wanted to get even with Neville Krendel. Well, that's not true. I knew Neville didn't kill Pam."

Abruptly, she broke off, made a dismissive gesture with her hand. "Anyway, it's all water under the bridge."

"I don't think so, Mrs. Dackers. Isn't this a classic example of the past finally catching up with the present?"

The other woman stared at her. Then, after a long pause, Mrs. Charles asked quietly, "How do you know that Neville Krendel didn't kill Mrs. Pym?"

Mrs. Dackers frowned at her cup. "Because I saw him, *Rendell*—I know what time he really came home that night. And it wasn't when he said. That man could tell a lie like no one I've ever known. He could make anyone believe anything he said." Her eyes narrowed maliciously. "Except that copper . . . Rendell slipped up badly there. Met up with himself face-to-face, didn't he?" She laughed bitterly. "The same rotten type."

"And you've never told anybody this before? That you could've given the lie to the time Rendell Pym claimed he came home?"

"No. And I'll deny I ever said it if you try to make something out of it. Pam only got what she deserved. She was a real little madam, I can tell you." Mrs. Dackers shrugged irritably. "What does it matter, anyway? Rendell's dead."

"Not according to Mr. Justice Halahan."

"That senile old fool," said Mrs. Dackers disparagingly. "You can't take any notice of anything that old goat said. He wouldn't have recognised Rendell. . . . Rendell suffered a severe nervous breakdown after he came back to Lymstead —you probably know all this—but, anyway, I was going to visit him once and Rosa—Mrs. Trumble—stopped me. The change in him, both in his personality and his appearance, was so dramatic I wouldn't recognise him, she said. And she didn't want him disturbed by too many reminders of the past. I didn't really want to see him like that, anyway—a broken shell."

Mrs. Dackers paused, shrugged. "The man I remembered was—" She broke off, eyes narrowed, and thought for a moment. "Exciting, virile. And yet . . . *primitive*. He was such a strong, vigorous man. Always a brute," she laughed shortly. "But a real *man*."

She lapsed into silence. After a minute or two, Mrs. Charles leaned forward to place her cup on the tray and asked quietly, "Why did you go to Tony Manners about the loss of your birds and accuse Neville Krendel of their theft?"

Mrs. Dackers looked at her quickly. "How do you know about that?"

Mrs. Charles ignored the question. "Was it purely out of pique again?"

Mrs. Dackers jumped to her feet, flung aside the towel. "My God," she stormed. "Everybody's the same. A business woman makes a perfectly legitimate accusation against a man she knows for a fact to be a liar and a thief and immediately everybody starts thinking, 'Oh yes, we know all about that, don't we? A woman scorned and getting her own back . . .' Well, all right. So I wasn't too thrilled about the way Neville and my daughter had been deceiving me behind my back—I admit that. But those birds were mine and he took them."

"He admitted it?"

"Yes. He claimed I owed him back pay. . . . He used to work for me—this was last year when I was living over in

Uppingham. In fact, I was thinking of making him a full partner when he and Tina, my daughter, up and disappeared together. I knew I hadn't a hope in hell of getting my birds back. However, when—coincidentally—a number of other breeders lost birds and we held a meeting about it, I suggested hiring a private investigator to look into the matter. I knew nothing would come of it—not so far as Neville was concerned—but I thought it might just teach him a lesson and that in the future he might think carefully before taking things that don't belong to him without first asking the owner's permission."

"There are a number of private inquiry agents listed in the Gidding telephone directory. What made you choose Tony Manners?"

Mrs. Dackers shrugged, sat down again. "I only wanted to scare Neville—I couldn't have cared less about the other breeders and their stupid birds. And I didn't think she'd be much good. I had no idea she'd been a policewoman. She never said. And I certainly didn't ask to see her credentials. I wasn't looking for anyone too bright, was I?"

"Did Tony mention that she remembered you and Neville Krendel from the Pym case?"

"No," said the other woman shortly. "We only ever discussed the missing birds." She laughed coldly. "That little madam was a lot shrewder than I thought. I knew nothing about her and the calls she used to make on Pam Pym after Rendell had come home and given her a good hiding until Neville told me who she was."

"Was he aware that Tony was unhappy with the Pym investigation?"

Mrs. Dackers frowned. "How do you mean? She didn't doubt that Rendell killed Pam, did she?"

"I don't know what she thought, Mrs. Dackers. Unfortunately, somebody—I believe—killed her before she could talk."

"You're joking," said Mrs. Dackers. A fearful look came into her eyes. "Who would want to kill her?"

"Whoever killed Mrs. Pym," replied the clairvoyante.

CHAPTER EIGHTEEN

Dolly Dackers hurried away down the road. She got into the white van, which had been left parked nearby, and then drove off quickly.

Mrs. Charles, who had stood in the doorway watching her visitor leave, remained there for some minutes longer pondering their conversation.

It wasn't because of either Benjamin Bing or John Ramsay that Dolly Dackers had come all the way out to the village from Lymstead to see her, which was what she was undoubtedly supposed to think. It was her visit to the Birdarama that morning. Dolly Dackers had been either sent by Neville Krendel to see what she could find out, or she had come of her own accord. With the same purpose in mind, of course.

Were they both, individually or collectively, simply worried because they would see an unpleasant episode in their lives being stirred up again? An episode from which both had emerged with little that could be said of either one of them to their credit. Mrs. Charles frowned musingly. They were hardly likely to display any more wisdom or behave any better in the present circumstances than they had then. . . .

Unless there was something they were afraid her present inquiries might lead her to discover about them. Or one of them . . . That Neville Krendel had murdered Pamela Pym?

But if Dolly Dackers had been telling the truth about knowing the time that Pym really came home that night and Pym therefore *had* murdered his wife, Purdie the publican hadn't perjured himself at Pym's trial, he had been telling the truth. In which case, it was later on that he had lied, after he knew that Fullbright had been transferred safely out of the area. Fullbright, being the kind of man he was, would have undoubtedly put pressure on Purdie at the time of the trial. But had that undue pressure he had allegedly brought to bear on Purdie been simply to get him to tell the truth?

Mrs. Charles's frown deepened. No, surely it was the first time round that Purdie had perjured himself. It was far more likely to be Dolly Dackers who was lying now to protect her former lover.

And yet if this were so, Mrs. Charles argued with herself, why hadn't Krendel suffered the same fate as Pym's three wise monkeys? If anything, Krendel should have been the first to go!

Why had the doctor, the judge, and the detective all fallen victims to Pym's vendetta and not the man whom Pym swore had murdered his wife?

Mrs. Charles shook her head perplexedly. Both Fullbright and Dolly Dackers were adamant that Pym had murdered his wife. But both of these witnesses were heavily prejudiced. One wanted a conviction (and as David had commented on Fullbright's attitude to Trevor Flegg, where Trevor currently fitted Fullbright's bill, so had Pym before him—the man everyone, and particularly, it seemed, Full-bright, had loved to hate). And in Dolly Dackers's case, she had simply wanted to protect her lover—and, for all anyone knew, was still protecting him, despite his deplorable treatment of her. Some women couldn't help themselves. . . .

Sighing a little, Mrs. Charles stepped back and slowly closed the door. Even David, she recalled, pausing momentarily, believed Pym guilty. Only W.P.C. Tony Manners had apparently been prepared to give Pym the benefit of the doubt. And when the two people whose further evidence ultimately resulted in the quashing of Pym's sentence abruptly stepped back into her life, those original doubts about who had really murdered Pamela Pym resurfaced.

Had Tony Manners died because of those doubts? Would

she be alive today if she hadn't taken a sudden personal interest in her one and only client, Dolly Dackers, and Neville Krendel?

And what of Ernest Hammond? Was he telling the truth when he claimed to have had no prior knowledge of the private file Tony had been keeping on these two people?

Had his name also been somewhere in that file?

Mrs. Charles's thoughts broke off midstream, her eyes narrowed. No, it wasn't necessarily Tony's interest in Dolly Dackers and Krendel (and Hammond, possibly) which had led to her abrupt death, it was the newspaper report on the judge, the account of how Halahan had died . . . her linking his death with what Mrs. Flegg had told her of the doctor's murder and then Tony's subsequent call on Benjamin Bing. Which could very well lead straight back to Dolly Dackers and Neville Krendel, thought Mrs. Charles with another sigh. Bing had told Dolly, Dolly had told Krendel. . . .

And Krendel had realised that Tony was onto him and he had done something about it?

But if Neville Krendel had murdered Tony, why, Mrs. Charles asked herself, had he murdered Dr. MacDonald, the judge, and attempted to murder the detective? It was too much of a coincidence that Fullbright's mouth had been covered with sticking plaster—he was definitely another victim of Pym's vendetta.

And what about Purdie? If it were Krendel and not Trevor Flegg who had attacked Fullbright, then surely it followed that Trevor Flegg hadn't murdered Purdie?

But Trevor's fingerprints were found on the murder weapon and there was some of Purdie's blood on his clothing. . . .

The telephone suddenly rang, but the call, which was being made from a pay phone, was cut off before anyone had a chance to speak.

A minute later the telephone rang again, and this time the caller got through.

"Mrs. Charles?" a woman's voice asked anxiously; and then, before the clairvoyante had a chance to reply, "You said to ring you. It's Enid Flegg here. Trev . . . He escaped from custody while he was appearing at court late this morning. He got away through an unlocked toilet window. The police came round not long ago looking for him, but I don't think they really expected to find him with me. They were after the names and addresses of any friends he's got down in London. They left as soon as I'd given them what they wanted. Trevor's only got the one friend that I know of in London—a Gidding lad he used to go to school with who's got a bed-sitter in Earl's Court. Or that's what he brags to Trev. More likely a cardboard carton underneath the arches somewhere."

"Is that where you expect Trevor will go?"

Mrs. Flegg hesitated. Then she said, "Yes, I think so. Eventually."

There was a strange little pause, as if both women knew there was something else to be said and each was waiting for the other to say it. At length, Mrs. Charles asked, "Do you know where Trevor is, Mrs. Flegg?"

"I—" Mrs. Flegg paused. Then, hesitatingly, "I'm not sure. I can't make up my mind, that's really why I phoned you, to ask your advice about what I should do. One of my neighbour's youngsters knocked on my door a little while ago with a telephone message from my sister—the one in Lymstead who's always ill. Liz wants me to go over there straightaway. And I'm to bring some money with me, she told my neighbour. That might sound odd to you, but it wouldn't if you knew my sister. I get very strange messages from her sometimes."

"But you think Trevor might be with her?"

Mrs. Flegg hesitated. Then, "No. You see, Liz isn't there. I went over last Saturday morning and saw her off myself. She was off to Jersey with a friend on a ten-day holiday. I know it's possible that she took ill while she was away and had to come home early, but I doubt it. Liz only *thinks* she's ill.

She's really as strong as a horse. And I've never known her to be ill at holiday time before. It's the only time I can count on her to be fighting fit."

She hesitated again. Then, falteringly, "Obviously it was a woman who phoned my neighbour."

Mrs. Flegg paused; the silence on the line grew heavy, lengthened. Then, with mounting panic, she finally unburdened herself of her real fear.

"Before I phoned you, I rang The Ugly Duckling—Mr. Purdie's pub. Ellen Purdie has gone missing. She disappeared soon after closing time after lunch today. The lady I spoke to there—the wife of the temporary manager the brewery has put in to look after things for the time being—told me that Ellen had a phone call from a boyfriend soon after they closed at three. Ellen never said who it was. Then somewhere around three-thirty she said she was going out for a while. She was supposed to be back for opening time at five, but she never showed up.

"I'm very sorry to burden you with all of this, Mrs. Charles, but I'm at my wits' end. Is it them—Trevor and Ellen—over there at my sister's? I know I should tell the police, but if it is genuinely Liz wanting me to go over, she'd had a fit if she suddenly found her place surrounded by police. And if you saw the carload who turned up just to get an address, you'd know what I'm talking about! It was quite frightening the way they stormed in. I wouldn't be a bit surprised if they went after Trev armed with guns. It's happening all the time these days, isn't it?"

Mrs. Flegg's voice caught up in a sob. "What if they shot him? How could I bear that on my conscience . . . knowing that I'd been the one who'd set them after him?"

"They won't do that, Mrs. Flegg," said the clairvoyante. "And it's most unlikely that they'll be armed when there's no reason for them to expect that your son is carrying a weapon." Mrs. Charles paused. Then, thoughtfully, "He hasn't got a gun, has he?"

Mrs. Flegg started to cry. "I can't find his father's gun—his old service revolver. Trev didn't come back to the flat today —I know that. I've been in all day. He must've taken it some other time and hidden it somewhere."

The pips went, and for a moment Mrs. Charles thought they had been cut off. Then she heard another coin being fed into the slot and Mrs. Flegg's voice asking, "What am I to do?"

"First and foremost," said the clairvoyante, "you must stop jumping to conclusions. You're only frightening yourself. Go back home and wait for me. I'll get there as soon as I can."

"Then what?" asked Mrs. Flegg.

"We'll do as your sister asks."

"But—"

Mrs. Flegg was cut off in mid protest.

"One step at a time, Mrs. Flegg," said the clairvoyante quietly. "Go home, speak to no one, and wait for me. And meanwhile, save your tears until you've got all the facts."

CHAPTER NINETEEN

It was dark and drizzling when the taxi pulled up outside the home of Mrs. Flegg's sister in Lymstead.

The house, a small, pebble-dashed semi, was in complete darkness.

"Something's wrong," said Mrs. Flegg as she and Mrs. Charles walked up to the front door. "Liz always leaves the porch light on when she knows I'm coming over late at night like this."

Mrs. Flegg rang the bell. The door opened almost immediately, just a crack, and a young girl's voice whispered anxiously, "Is that you, Mrs. Flegg?"

"Ellen?" responded Mrs. Flegg.

The door opened wide. "You'd better come in quickly," said Ellen Purdie. "We can't switch on the lights. Somebody might be watching. Trev's out the back in the kitchen waiting for you. Did you bring the money?"

The girl's eyes widened with fear as she looked past Mrs. Flegg and saw Mrs. Charles. "Who's she?"

Trevor Flegg suddenly appeared at the end of the shadowy hall. "Mum? Did you bring the money?" He stiffened. "Who's that with you?"

"A friend," replied his mother.

"Is there somewhere we can talk?" asked Mrs. Charles.

Trevor rounded on his mother explosively. "A bleedin' social worker! You've brought a social worker with you!"

"No, Trev," said his mother quickly. "Mrs. Charles is a private investigator. You remember Tony Manners—I used to clean for her. Mrs. Charles has been hired to investigate Tony's death. That's how we met—"

"What's she doing here, then?"

"She's promised to help us."

"We don't need anybody's help," said Trevor. "I know how to take care of myself. Give me the money you brought, and Ellen and me'll be on our way. They'll never find us where we're going."

"I would imagine that the police are already one step ahead of you and are waiting for you in London," said Mrs. Charles. "That's if you were thinking of heading straight for your friend's bedsitter in Earl's Court."

Trevor scowled at his mother. "You told them."

"I had to, Trev. They came round late this afternoon, and I had to give them Berni's address. I had no option. They seemed to know that you'd head straight for London."

"I told you they would," said Ellen Purdie miserably. "Give yourself up, Trev. You're only making things worse."

"Don't you start," he growled.

"I want to go home," said Ellen.

"Go on, then," he said. "Nobody's stopping you."

He spun round on his heel and went swiftly down the hall to the kitchen, then switched on the light. Everyone followed him.

Kicking out a chair from the table, he flopped down on it moodily.

"Somebody'll see the light on and think there are burglars in here," said Ellen fearfully. "They might phone the police."

"So what?" he said. "The old lady's as good as shopped me anyhow."

"You give up easily, don't you?" observed Mrs. Charles.

He scowled at her.

"It's always like that with you, isn't it? The slightest obstacle—and I suspect you yourself deliberately place them in your path so you'll have an excuse not to follow through with your plans—and that's it, you give up. Like the robbery you planned to carry out at The Ugly Duckling—if, that is, Ellen would leave the front door unlocked for you. You're defeated before you even begin, Trevor Flegg. And you're the one who does the defeating, you and you alone. You don't need any help from anybody else here. Certainly not from your mother, nor from Ellen."

Trevor flung her a venomous look.

Ellen said nervously, "How do you know that Trev planned to rob my dad?"

"That's not important. Just be thankful that I do know. Right now it's about the only thing you, Trevor, have got going for you."

He looked at her contemptuously.

Ellen was beginning to look very afraid. "If she tells the police that, Trev—"

"The police," he sneered. "What do they know?"

"What happened to your father's gun, Trevor?" asked Mrs. Flegg. "You've got it, haven't you?"

He shrugged and shuffled his feet.

Ellen stared at him, horrified. "You never said anything to me about a gun. . . . Where is it?"

He smiled smugly. "Never you mind."

"Don't be a fool, Trev," she said, her voice rising a little with fear.

He got suddenly to his feet and strode to the door which gave onto the back garden. "I'm getting out of here, I've had enough of this. Nag, nag, nag—that's all you women ever do."

"Where's he going?" asked Ellen anxiously as the door slammed behind him. "He hasn't any money."

"Then he'll be back," said the clairvoyante. She drew out a chair and sat down.

Mrs. Flegg and Ellen stared at her. "What do we do now?" asked Mrs. Flegg.

"We wait," said Mrs. Charles.

Mrs. Flegg and Ellen exchanged glances and then, after hesitating momentarily, they too sat down.

Mrs. Charles said to Ellen, "I am very sorry about your father."

"We weren't close," said the girl with a shrug. "He wasn't my real father. My mother remarried when I was three."

"Has The Ugly Duckling always been your home? Since your mother married Mr. Purdie, I mean?"

The girl nodded. "Yes. Mum never liked it . . . me being about the pub when I was little. But there wasn't much she could do about it. Dad—Mr. Purdie—promised her he was going to give up the place once they got married—he knew how much she hated it there—but he never really meant it. He never kept any of his promises."

"Is your mother alive?"

Ellen shook her head.

Mrs. Flegg said, "Mrs. Purdie was one of Rosa Trumble's patients for a time."

"When was this?" asked Mrs. Charles.

Mrs. Flegg looked at Ellen, who said, "A long time ago. I was only eight. Mum had a nervous breakdown—this was what I was told later, when I was old enough to understand. All I can remember is that Mum suddenly started acting strange, saying weird things about Dad—Mr. Purdie. It was awful—I couldn't understand what was going on. She kept packing and unpacking our suitcases and telling me I had to keep it a secret, we were going to run away as soon as Dad wasn't looking. Well, actually, it wasn't Dad she was running away from. She kept saying he was somebody else, not Dad. It was very frightening. Soon after that she went into the nursing home."

"Did you ever visit her there?"

"Only once. And then I was so upset afterwards that Mrs. Trumble told Dad it would be best if I didn't go there again. Mum thought they were trying to kill her—Dad and Mrs. Trumble, this is—so she couldn't tell anybody that he wasn't the man she'd married. It was really scary. Mum frightened me."

"You were afraid she'd harm you physically?"

"No. It was the things she used to say. Like how they were going to poison her, and that once they'd got rid of her they'd come after me and kill me too. And I wasn't to trust them."

"How long ago did she die?"

The girl shrugged. "I'm not sure. It wasn't long after I went to see her. . . . I was about ten, then, I think, so that'd be about eight years ago. They told me—at least Dad did eventually—that Mum had been hiding her tablets, and then, when she'd got enough, she swallowed them all at once and killed herself."

"Forgive me for asking you all these questions, Ellen," said the clairvoyante quietly. "I know it must be very distressing for you, but it's very important for Trevor's sake, though I can't take you into my confidence at this stage and tell you why. Just trust me and believe me when I say you're helping Trevor and Mrs. Flegg."

Ellen nodded. "I don't mind you asking about Mum, honestly. It was a long time ago."

"Do you know how long your mother was a patient at The Grange?"

"Not really. She was in and out of other hospitals—ordinary ones—before she went to The Grange. That seemed to go on for ages. . . . I mean, after she first started to act a bit strange. Then finally Dad said she was getting a lot better and that she could soon be home for good. But first she'd have to go to The Grange—he said it was a sort of convalescent home—for a while." Ellen shrugged. "She—Mum—didn't seem better to me when I saw her. I thought she was getting worse."

"Did your mother speak of any of the other patients when you went to see her?"

The girl shook her head. "No, not really. Not that I remember, anyway. Dad and Mrs. Trumble were the only people she mentioned. As a matter of fact, I wasn't really sure she knew who I was. She suddenly started calling me Pamela and asked if I'd come to see Rendell. . . . That was one of the other patients there—a friend of Dad's."

"Rendell Pym?"

"Did you know him?" asked the girl. Then, without waiting for an answer, "It was all that trouble over Mr. Pym that pushed Mum into a breakdown. I reckon it was, anyway. She was very upset about it . . . when Mr. Pym murdered his wife and Dad got himself and the pub mixed up in it. It was awful. I can still remember hearing Mum yell and scream at him about it. They had terrible rows over it. She thought it was awful—you know, that Dad's best friend was a murderer."

"But Mr. Pym wasn't a murderer," Mrs. Charles pointed out. "He was acquitted."

"Yes, I know. Dad told me. But he still did it. I heard Dad say so."

"He told your mother this?"

The girl nodded.

The back door suddenly opened and Trevor walked in. There was a revolver tucked into the waistband of his jeans. He strode through the kitchen and into the hall without a word.

Mrs. Flegg got up as if to follow him, but Mrs. Charles stopped her. "Let me try and talk to him," she suggested.

The clairvoyante found Trevor in the living room peering through a slit in the curtains at the street.

"I don't think there's anybody there," she said. "But if you wait around long enough, something's bound to happen that will get you off the hook. The neighbours probably . . . With a bit of luck they'll have seen the kitchen light and have phoned the police. And that'll be another problem taken care of for you, won't it?"

"Think you're clever, don't you?" he snarled, striding past her and defiantly switching on the light. "Just like the cops. They think they know it all too."

"With good reason, I'd say," she said. "What with your fingerprints on the murder weapon and the murder victim's blood on your clothes."

"I didn't kill Purdie. I didn't mug that other old geezer neither."

"Don't tell me, tell them," said the clairvoyante.

"Yeah," he said. "Fat chance I'd have of them believing anything I said. I wouldn't waste my breath. Might just as well do my porridge and forget it. They're going to get me for this, anyway. Why should I make their job easier? I've no previous convictions," he shrugged. "I reckon I could get off lightly."

"You have to be one of the most charitable people I've ever met, or the most stupid," remarked the clairvoyante.

Trevor shrugged again, smirked. "But nowhere near as stupid as the cops."

"Is that a general comment or are you speaking specifically of Mr. Purdie's murder?"

He shrugged, didn't answer.

"Why are they stupid, Trevor?" She hesitated, studied his face closely. He was so determined to be a victim that it was difficult to tell whether he was being smug or merely self-pitying. Just occasionally, his attitude was definitely smug, as if he had good cause to consider the police inferior to himself and was enjoying this feeling of superiority.

"You know something about Mr. Purdie, don't you? Something the police don't know," she guessed.

He looked at her quickly, looked down at his feet, shuffled them.

"Be sensible, Trevor," she said quietly. "If not for your own sake, then for your mother's. If you do know something, or if you saw something that the police have missed and you're deliberately not telling them what it was, it's the real killer who's the clever one, not you. You're letting him use you to prove how clever *he* is. Your quarrel isn't really with the police at all, you know. It's with him. You see, Trevor, he's killed before. In fact, I believe Mr. Fullbright and Mr. Purdie were his fifth and sixth victims. Although he wasn't quite so successful where Mr. Fullbright was concerned."

Mrs. Charles paused. Trevor was still staring at his feet and shuffling them, but he was listening to her. She went on.

"This may be very hard for you to believe, Trevor, but the

trouble you find yourself in now all began approximately eleven years ago when you were still a small boy. First with the murder of a woman named Pamela Pym, then with the murder of a Dr. MacDonald, next came a Crown Court judge, followed by the death of a former woman police officer—Tony Manners—and then finally the attack on Mr. Fullbright and the murder of Mr. Purdie."

While she had been speaking, Trevor had looked up slowly at her. Frowning, he said, "Mum used to work for a Dr. MacDonald."

The clairvoyante nodded.

The youth's frown deepened. "The police never said anything about the others." He suddenly looked alarmed. "I didn't have nothing to do with them. . . . Dr. MacDonald was a good bloke. I liked him."

"You might have difficulty proving that, particularly as your mother once worked for him. You know how things can get distorted, Trevor. Some minor grievance you might have once had with the doctor while you and your mother were living under his roof could be recalled and suddenly assume quite different proportions. . . ."

Mrs. Charles was silent for a moment. Then, continuing, "I think I can understand how you must be feeling. I too was once accused of a serious crime which I didn't commit. You might think you're being clever. You may even see it as something of a joke. And if that is the case, Trevor, then it's a joke at your expense. The police aren't complete fools, you know. They will eventually discover what it was that they missed. And then what? If they have any reason at all to suspect that you've been deliberately obstructing their inquiries by withholding this information—"

"They didn't miss it."

Trevor was still inclined to be sullen, but the clairvoyante knew that he was worried and that he would tell her now what she wanted to know. He went on grudgingly.

"You've got it all back to front. And I dunno why you keep on about Purdie," he mumbled crossly. "It didn't have nothing to do with him. It was afterwards—after he told us to push off. We—me and my mates—were larking about outside his pub, and he came out and told us to clear off or he'd call out the pigs. So we started to walk home, didn't we? At least I did . . . through the Hydebank Open Space."

The clairvoyante looked at him inquiringly.

"Some people call it the common," he explained in a grumbling voice. "But it's really the Hydebank Open Space." He frowned at her as if she were a backward child who was having difficulty in keeping up with him. "Where that old geezer was mugged and the dog was killed. Me and my mates split up there, and that was the way I started to walk home—through the Hydebank Open Space."

CHAPTER TWENTY

David Sayer was appalled. He was not in the least interested in Trevor Flegg's story, dismissed it as being of no account, and went straight for what he considered to be the more important issue.

"You mean you knowingly aided and abetted a fugitive on the run? Really, Madame. You've gone too far this time!"

"He promised me he'd give himself up to the police," said the clairvoyante imperturbably. "I doubt that they'll find him any more cooperative than he's been in the past. But he will give himself up, Superintendent."

He regarded her sceptically. "And you believed him?"

"He'll probably take his time about it. But yes, I think he'll keep his word." She smiled faintly. "The martyr in him will see to that." Her expression became serious. "Trevor was, I think, telling me the truth about that night, Superintendent. He did not attack and rob Fullbright—I am absolutely certain of that—and there is only a very slight possibility that he killed Purdie."

"And the little matter of his fingerprints on the murder weapon?"

"He admitted he handled it—and Purdie's body. This was how he came to get his blood on his clothes. But Trevor says —and I'm inclined to believe him—that Purdie was already dead. Trevor told me he went back to The Ugly Duckling that night hoping to see Ellen Purdie, and he found Purdie lying sprawled out facedown on the ground out the back of the premises. At first he thought Purdie had had another heart attack—apparently Purdie had a history of heart trouble. So Trevor rolled him over onto his back to see if he were still alive. That was how he got Purdie's blood on his clothes and why he touched the murder weapon which, he said, Purdie was lying on. Then, as soon as he realised what had really happened, he became frightened and got away as quickly as he could. Only this time he caught a bus home to Gidding.

"Earlier, when Purdie had moved him on from outside the pub, he had intended to cut across the common and spend the night at his aunt's . . . something he told me he often does when he goes over to Lymstead hoping to see Ellen Purdie after closing time. However, in this instance he'd forgotten for the moment that his aunt had gone away on holiday. Then, when he remembered, he decided to chance risking Purdie's wrath and turned back to the pub to see Ellen."

"Very well, then," said David. "Flegg's telling the truth, the whole truth, and nothing but the truth. Who, then, attacked Fullbright and then killed Purdie?"

"The same person who killed Pamela Pym."

David sighed. "Rendell Pym . . . A dead man. Or had you forgotten that small detail?"

"Are you really so sure that Rendell Pym murdered his wife?"

"Beyond all reasonable doubt, Madame," said David firmly.

Mrs. Charles thought for a moment. Then she nodded. "Very well, just for argument's sake, we'll say that Rendell Pym it is. . . . And Rendell Pym it was—who attacked Fullbright and murdered Purdie, that is. And again, just for argument's sake, we'll say he's still alive—as I think I might've suggested to you once before."

David was shaking his head. "Fullbright identified his body."

"The same man also admitted that Pym was cunning— one of the most artfully sly, cunning villains he'd ever come up against, he said. He also said that the body of the man he identified as being Rendell Pym was a mess. Therefore, so long as that body was dressed in Pym's clothing with his identification on him, just about anyone with a modicum of intelligence would have been able to identify him."

"Fullbright wouldn't make that kind of mistake."

"That wasn't the impression you gave me from what you said the other day about his attitude to Trevor Flegg. This was just like everything else. That body on the railway line fitted the bill. He wanted Pym dead."

David sighed. "All right . . . So Fullbright isn't the brightest of specimens."

"Then so far so good. We are agreed on at least that point. Now let us take my supposition one step further. What if Rendell Pym has undergone an even more dramatic metamorphosis than the one Fullbright witnessed while Pym was one of Rosa Trumble's patients? Maybe Rendell Pym was, *is*, every bit as great an actor as people say—Fullbright in particular. Remember what he told us of Pym's impersonation of his sister one year at the home's Christmas party?"

Mrs. Charles looked at David steadily for a moment. Then, smiling faintly, she went on, "I think Rendell Pym was acting from the moment he stepped over Rosa Trumble's threshold until the day finally came for him to make his first move against the people he'd sworn to revenge himself upon."

"He took his time about it," observed David in a dry voice. "What was holding him back?"

She smiled. "Rosa Trumble. She, I believe, is the key to the whole mystery. Or more precisely, the closure of her nursing home. This enabled Pym to act. To fake his death so that he could then move freely among his intended victims and kill them off one by one as he had vowed."

David shook his head. "I'm sorry, Madame. Pym is dead."

"Can you—the police—prove that to me? Do the police still have Pym's fingerprints on record? Will they be in a position to compare them with those of the person whom I suspect might be Rendell Pym and tell me I'm wrong?"

"You ask that question as if you already know the answer,

Madame," observed David. "No. Pym's fingerprints would've been destroyed when he was acquitted. It's the law. As I suspect you very well know."

She smiled, and after a moment he too smiled. Then he said, "Did I hear right or do my ears deceive me? The person you suspect only *might* be Pym. You've actually got *doubts?*"

"It all really rather depends on whether or not Trevor Flegg is telling the truth," she admitted. Then, smiling again, "You see, Superintendent, if Trevor Flegg killed Purdie, then Purdie was really Rendell Pym—Pym having murdered Purdie (the real Purdie) some years ago and then stepped into his shoes. And then in that case, what happened on Tuesday night was this. . . .

"Pym, alias Purdie, escorted three young men from his premises somewhere around 10 P.M. (I was talking to Ellen Purdie on the phone shortly before you arrived, and she has filled in all these details for me.) Pym/Purdie, according to Ellen, was gone for some time, reappearing only a short while before closing time at ten-thirty. Ellen recalls that he suddenly came into the public bar rolling down his shirt sleeves. She also noticed that his forearms looked wet—as if he'd had a wash and hadn't taken the time to dry himself properly, and she wondered to herself where he'd been. Ellen listed a number of jobs outside or down in the cellar that he could've been seeing to, to which, possibly, could be added the attack on Fullbright and his dog. Which, perhaps coincidentally, Purdie—in common with Pym—disliked intensely, according to Ellen."

David gave her a wry look. "Purdie saw off the lads, ducked across the road to the common, clubbed the dog and Fullbright (hopefully) to death, and then nipped back to the pub in time to give himself a quick wash and brushup before calling last orders? A busy man, Madame!"

"It could all have been accomplished in less than fifteen minutes, Superintendent."

He grunted noncommittally. "Then what?" he asked.

"The lads Pym/Purdie had seen off started larking about,

so he went out to send them on their way, leaving Ellen to lock up after him as he intended to come in the back way. After he had made sure that the lads had gone, he went round the back of the premises. However, while he was out there, Trevor returned, they argued, and Trevor—in what can only be described as an ironic twist of fate—picked up the piece of wood which Pym/Purdie had used in his attack on Fullbright and the dog (and which Pym/Purdie had obviously left lying about out there when he went out earlier) and killed him with it."

"H'm," said David. "I find it hard to believe that Ellen didn't spot something odd about her dad if—as you've suggested—Pym did swap places with him."

Mrs. Charles smiled at his scepticism. "Ah, but she did notice something odd about him. And what's more, her mother maintained that Purdie wasn't the man she'd married. This was shortly before Mrs. Purdie became a patient of Rosa Trumble's. . . ."

Mrs. Charles smiled at the sudden look David shot at her. She went straight on, "In fact, Mrs. Purdie accused Rosa Trumble and Purdie of plotting to kill her. Ultimately she died of a drug overdose. Suicide was the official verdict."

"Rosa Trumble again, eh?" he said slowly.

"Ellen also spoke today on the phone of the changes she'd noticed in Purdie's personality, particularly his intense irritability, which she attributed to his heart trouble. She'd already told me they weren't close, but I thought it rather interesting when she remarked at one point during our phone conversation today that he was one of those people who aren't really capable of being loving, or of having a loving relationship with anyone."

"That's more or less what Fullbright said about Pym." David frowned, looked at her thoughtfully. "You're building up quite a case there, Madame."

She looked at him for a moment. Then she said, "It's got its flaws, but I'm working on them."

"But if Flegg is telling the truth . . . If he didn't murder Purdie?"

"Then a dangerous psychopath is still at large, Superintendent. A man that must be caught and caught quickly."

"Not by Merton he won't be. Not this time." David shook his head. "He'd never believe a word of this."

"Then we'll just have to do it all by ourselves, won't we?"

"How?"

"Quite easily, Superintendent." She smiled at him. "We're going to hold a seance."

He stared at her.

"It's the only solution, believe me," she assured him. "If Rendell Pym is still alive, then that is the way to catch him out. In this instance, dead men will quite literally tell tales. But first," she went on briskly, "there's a little errand I'd like you to run for me, if you wouldn't mind, and I have a number of phone calls still to make. There's just one little point I have to clear up."

"Only one?" he said dryly. Then, "A seance? With a medium? *You?*"

She laughed, shook her head. "Good heavens, no. I've got somebody really special all lined up there, Superintendent. I'm sure you'll find it most interesting."

I can hardly wait, he thought uneasily.

CHAPTER TWENTY-ONE

The chief superintendent's face went a deeper shade of red. A thick, bluish purple vein stood out on his forehead.

"She did *what?*" he said. Then, when David Sayer prepared to go through it all again, "No, don't bother, I heard you the first time. I'll have her for this, Dave, I swear it! She's gone too far this time."

"That was what I told her. But the lad turned himself in, didn't he? You'd still be searching for him down in London's bed-sitter land if it hadn't been for her intervention."

David looked across Merton's desk at him, smiled. "I warned her you wouldn't be pleased. I even told her I wasn't going to tell you about it."

"So what made you change your mind?" sneered Merton. "Once a copper, eh?"

"No, as a matter of fact it was the lad—when he gave himself up. She said he would and I thought she was mad. So if she was right there, maybe she'll be right about the rest of it."

"Your faith in her is most touching," snarled Merton. "I'm sure your wife must think so too."

David smiled at the pointed barb. "Jean's her biggest fan. Like you said, I'll always be a copper."

"So you're not a hundred precent with her this time, eh?" Merton eyed him shrewdly. His high colour began to subside, and he smiled to himself. Madame Marvellous couldn't be right all the time, everybody made mistakes. And by heaven! She'd made one this time, he could feel it in his bones. "Well?" he said.

David shrugged. Then, after a moment, "What's the lad got to say for himself—anything?"

"Not a dicky-bird. Just sits and grins. Like some other people I could mention who've come under the doubtful influence of Madame Marvellous."

Merton leaned back in his chair, regarded David speculatively for a moment or two. Then he said, "Okay, so what is it this time? I take it that for some reason best known to herself, she's decided to champion young Flegg's cause and that in the furtherance of that aim she's got something special in mind."

"Er, yes," said David. "As a matter of fact she has. A seance."

"Very nice too," said Merton. "What's a seance got to do with laddie?"

"Nothing really. It's Purdie she's after. His ghost, I think. Or maybe it's Pym's. I'm not really sure."

"Pym who?"

"Rendell Pym. That chap over in Lymstead who—"

"I know," interrupted Merton. His eyes narrowed. "Go on."

"Purdie was the publican who perjured himself at Pym's trial."

"That's a fact?" said Merton. Then, after a small pause, "Well, go on, I'm listening. . . ."

"Martin Fullbright was in charge of the police investigation—"

"Really?" Merton's tone was very dry. "You learn something new every day."

David hesitated. Then he said, "I hope you'll take this the right way, Clive, but are you sure Flegg killed Purdie?"

Merton nodded his head slowly.

"Well, then, if you're right (and I hesitate to mention this, but I don't really think Mrs. Charles agrees with you), but if you're right, then she thinks there's a possibility that Purdie is—was—really Rendell Pym."

David grinned self-consciously. "I know it sounds crazy,

Clive, but she reckons Pym faked his death a couple of years back. The way she sees it, Pym murdered Purdie and then stepped into his shoes and systematically went about killing the chief prosecution witnesses and the judge at his trial, and a former W.P.C., Tony Manners, only to be killed himself by young Flegg in some stupid domestic row over Ellen Purdie. The W.P.C., by the way, was involved with the Pyms only incidentally, but Mrs. Charles thinks she tumbled to what was going on and had to be got rid of. But all of this is only if Flegg killed Purdie. If he didn't kill him, then Mrs. Charles has apparently got an altogether different theory about Pym."

Merton stared at David. Then he said softly, "By George! You know I really do believe I've got her this time. I can't miss!"

"Yes, very probably," admitted David. "I really think she's let herself get obsessed with this one. However, before you get too carried away, it might be an idea to check back on one curious coincidence that she's turned up where the deaths of the former W.P.C. and one of the prosecution witnesses and the judge—who was Halahan, by the way— are concerned. Mrs. Charles claims that in all three instances an elderly man with a strong accent of one kind or another was on or about the scene of the crime. I promised her I'd see what I could do about checking up on the old boy—an American tourist—who found the body of one of the witnesses, but there's an even quicker and simpler way now of proving whether or not Mrs. Charles is onto something. That old boy—the jogger—who stumbled across Fullbright first thing in the morning . . . I don't suppose he's got a funny accent, by any chance?"

Merton looked at him steadily. "Would that be funny ha-ha, or funny peculiar?"

"Unusual. Something pronounced. Like a Scots or American accent."

Merton's eyes narrowed meditatively. "Madame Marvellous's case stands or falls on this point, does it?"

"Well no. I wouldn't go so far as to say that. I'd just feel a little happier in my own mind if you were able to tell me—"

"That he's vanished into thin air?"

"If it wouldn't be too much to hope," David rejoined with a faint smile.

Merton picked up the telephone receiver and a second or two later barked, "That newspaper young Peters was reading when I came in a while ago. Fetch it in here, will you?"

Almost as Merton replaced the receiver, there was a tap on the door, and a young constable came in with a copy of that morning's edition of the *Sketch* and handed it to him.

Merton pushed it across the desk towards David and pointed to the photograph on the front page of the first runner over seventy years of age to cross the finishing line in the twenty-six mile marathon Gidding run, which had been held over the weekend.

"That's him, is it?" asked David, looking up from the newspaper.

"The one and only," said Merton. "Looks substantial enough to me," he added.

"No accent?"

"Only a local one. Nothing to write home about." He paused, looked at David for a moment. Then, with a smile, "Anything else I can do for you while you're here?"

"Er," said David. He hesitated, frowned. "This seance I mentioned. Mrs. Charles wanted me to fix something up for her with the security firm I occasionally do a bit of work for, but now that you're in on this, it'd probably be better, I think, if you provided us with the necessary."

"Her wish is my command," said Merton. He drew a notepad towards him, picked up a pencil, and then looked at David expectantly.

This, thought David, is too easy. Merton was being too nice. It wasn't natural. "Is Rutherford still about the place?" asked David cautiously. "He'd do nicely."

"Oh, we can do better than that. I've just the lad. Handles

old Mrs. Hawkins a treat. Mrs. Charles should be child's play by comparison."

David gave him a wary look. "Who's Mrs. Hawkins?"

"Trust me," said Merton.

David repeated his question.

Merton shrugged. "Oh, just some old dear who has a problem with men. Keeps finding them in her bedroom late at night and sends for us to see them off. They sit on the foot of her bed leering at her. Only they're not really there, if you know what I mean. It's a fixation, you see. Mrs. Hawkins sees leering males, and Mrs. Charles sees murderers."

"Something tells me you're not entering into this in the proper spirit."

"Perish the thought," said Merton. "And to prove how pure my motives are, if it's Rutherford and Bristowe you want (you do know they're a team, the two go together, don't you?), then so be it. Only too happy to be of service. Anything else I can do for you?"

David hesitated. He had been going to give Merton Trevor Flegg's account of his activities on the night that Purdie had been murdered, but he changed his mind. It was probably all a pack of lies, anyway. And there was no sense spoiling the man. Merton had already been given more than enough to laugh about for one day.

"Just one thing," said David. "Know anybody by the name of Valentine—Jimmy Valentine?"

Merton considered him for a moment before replying. "Maybe. He's not mixed up in this nonsense, is he?"

David didn't answer.

"Oh dear," said Merton.

"What's that supposed to mean?"

Merton began to chuckle. "So she's human after all. Never mind, it happens to the best of us sooner or later."

David gave him a rueful look. "He's a con man?"

"Amongst other things. Sucked her right in, has he? Shame," said Merton, straight-faced.

"You've got a vicious streak in you, Clive," said David.
"Yes. Awful, isn't it?"

Mrs. Charles smiled to herself at the concern she could hear in David Sayer's voice, which was more for himself than for her, she suspected.

"Anyway," he continued, "I wanted you to know that I changed my mind and went to see Merton. And I thought I really ought to phone and let you know as quickly as possible that your mysterious Mr. Valentine is a known confidence trickster."

"Thank you for telling me," she responded. "And I'm actually rather relieved about Mr. Merton."

"You don't seem terribly surprised," he commented. "About Valentine, that is."

"I did tell you that Charles the Third was a confidence man, didn't I?"

"Er, no, Madame. I don't believe you have mentioned that before. I thought he was the circus performer."

"A man of many guises, Superintendent. Well," she said. "Is Mr. Merton with us?"

"You're still going ahead?"

"Of course. Everything's fixed for tomorrow night at the Gidding branch of the Lymstead Spiritualists' Society."

"I'll tell Merton," said David, without too much enthusiasm. He hesitated. Then, "There was just one other thing, Madame. The jogger who raised the alarm about Fullbright . . . No accent of any consequence. He's a local man. And if you've got a copy of this morning's edition of the *Sketch* handy, that's him on the front page—the string bean in the jazzy athletic shorts and singlet. He's something of an ancient monument in and around Lymstead where he lives—everybody knows him. Which sort of queers things a bit for you, doesn't it? I mean, now that you know he's a genuine twenty-four carat, bona fide witness—no hanky-panky there."

"Oh no, Superintendent. Quite the reverse." She hesitated, smiled to herself. "You will be there tomorrow night, won't you?"

"Of course," he said.

In for a penny, he thought wryly to himself, in for a pound!

CHAPTER TWENTY-TWO

The secretary and treasurer of the Gidding branch of the Lymstead Spiritualists' Society, Mrs. Grace Goodbody, a late–middle-aged woman with a booming sergeant major's voice, was anxious that the clairvoyante and her invited guests should be fully cognisant with the society's procedures. Mr. Ramsay, Mrs. Goodbody explained, was one of the most naturally gifted mediums she personally had ever known; and being highly sensitive, he was therefore all too easily emotionally disturbed. Which, she stressed, depending on the extent of his distress at any one time, could be an extremely traumatic and consequently dangerous experience for him. Untold damage, she boomed, fixing everyone in turn with a steely eye, could be done should Mr. Ramsay fall deeply unconscious, with the tragic result that he might very well never be the same man again.

Their Mrs. Traynor, she added, was nowhere near as gifted as Mr. Ramsay, but she was definitely better emotionally equipped and could transport herself from one side to the other with none of the terrible side effects which poor Mr. Ramsay was obliged to suffer. However, as Madame Herrmann (and every time Mrs. Goodbody addressed Mrs. Charles thus, she all but came to attention and saluted) had asked expressly for Mr. Ramsay, then both she and Mr. Ramsay were only too pleased and honoured to oblige. Though, of course, with Mr. Ramsay having been slightly acquainted in a way in this life with the spirit form which Madame Herrmann wished to contact on the other side, it was only sensible that it should be he who would conduct the seance tonight.

Mrs. Goodbody further explained that while she could be thought of as an unnecessary outside influence, particularly as she would be the only person present at the seance who did not have some intimate knowledge of or past connection with the spirit of Rendell Maxwell Pym, her presence was nevertheless absolutely essential to Mr. Ramsay's well-being. All the more so since the prescribed ideal number of eight persons present at a seance had been exceeded in this instance (most unwisely, in her own personal opinion).

"The poor dear man," she finished, "does have such a difficult time of it. He simply must have someone whom he knows intimately and whom he can trust to guide him safely back into the light if something goes wrong."

Mrs. Goodbody then left the main hall while she went to see if Mr. Ramsay, who had gone quietly into a small anteroom to prepare himself for the seance, was ready to begin.

Mrs. Charles and her guests were seated on a platform round a large table. Mrs. Flegg, looking pale and tense, sat on the clairvoyante's left, next to Martin Fullbright. David Sayer sat on the other side of Mrs. Charles, and on his right was Ernest Hammond. Neville Krendel, thin-lipped and without his pipe (which the sergeant major had ordered him to remove from the hall the instant she had spied it), sat next to Hammond. Next to Krendel was Dolly Dackers. Benjamin Bing sat between her and Jimmy Valentine, who looked, thought David, every bit as grey and shadowy as he had imagined him.

With perhaps the exception of Mrs. Flegg and himself, David was surprised at the resignation he could see on the faces about him. The politician in Hammond, of course, he thought wryly, would want to get this business over and done with as quickly and with as little fuss as possible; and for one reason or another that probably applied to the rest of them, he guessed.

His gaze ranged slowly round the table. Krendel, the delectable Dolly, Benjamin Bing—they were all spiritualists (even Hammond it seemed, in a minor way, which still surprised David whenever he thought about it); and this, he could well see, might also account for a certain sense of inevitability about some things which someone else—someone who did not share their beliefs—might lack.

The two vacant seats around the table would eventually be taken up by Mrs. Goodbody and the medium, John Ramsay.

Mrs. Flegg, in a very low voice, said abruptly, "I'm afraid I'm beginning to feel a little faint. Do you think he will be very much longer?"

Mrs. Charles gave her an encouraging smile and then, keeping her own voice equally low, she said, "You'll feel much better once we begin. Just breathe deeply and try to relax. It shouldn't be long now."

Mrs. Flegg glanced uneasily at the man sitting next to her. "It will be all right, won't it?" she asked Mrs. Charles. "They'll let Trevor go. . . ."

"I hope so, Mrs. Flegg," replied the clairvoyante.

Suddenly, Fullbright said in a loud voice, "I remember Rosa, my sister, saying that this fellow's good."

Mrs. Charles put a cautionary finger to her lips, and he lowered his voice accordingly. "Sorry," he grumbled. "I forgot."

"Have you ever attended a seance before, Mr. Fullbright?" she inquired.

"No," he said in a hoarse whisper. "Rosa knew better than to ask me along. This side of it, spiritualism, is all a load of bunkum as far as I'm concerned. Nothing in it! You only got me here tonight because I knew Rosa'd never let me hear the end of it if Mrs. Dackers or Ramsay wrote to her about the seance and told her I wouldn't cooperate. Spirit healing —like Rosa used to do—is something quite different in my book. You can see the living, breathing proof of its existence." The old man bared his ghastly false teeth in a wide grin. "Though I've yet to see another spirit healer who could hold a candle to her."

Mrs. Charles cast a quick glance at Benjamin Bing, but he

sat as if made of stone, staring straight ahead of him without blinking.

"You met Mr. Ramsay once, didn't you?" the clairvoyante whispered to Fullbright.

He nodded. "Yes, I called in to their meeting place over in Lymstead one night to let everyone know how Rosa was getting on out in Australia, and he came up to me and made himself known."

Mrs. Charles nodded thoughtfully, then switched her gaze across the table to Dolly Dackers. So much depended on her. Pym had fooled Fullbright, but would he fool her? She had a decided advantage over the former police officer. Fullbright's relationship with Pym had been that of police officer and murder suspect; and that was how Fullbright had always seen Pym, strictly within the restrictive confines of that particular framework. But Dolly Dackers had known Pym in ordinary, everyday circumstances, without Fullbright's brand of prejudice, and had even been Pym's lover for a time. Would that give her an edge over Fullbright? When, *if,* the time came, would she succeed where Fullbright had failed and see through Pym's disguise?

Lights in the centre and at the back of the hall were suddenly switched off, leaving the raised platform on which everyone was seated with only a minimum of lighting from a single, plastic-shaded light bulb positioned directly above the table.

"Looks like this is it," murmured David.

"Pym did murder his wife, you know," said Fullbright in a strange, faintly disgruntled voice.

"Yes, I know that now," replied the clairvoyante. "That isn't what I wish to ask Rendell Pym tonight, Mr. Fullbright. I'm sorry if you've been led to believe that the purpose of this seance has anything to do with disproving your findings on Pym."

"Oh. That's all right, then," grunted Fullbright, mollified. "I just didn't like to think that—"

"*Sssh!*" said Dolly Dackers sharply. "Remember what

Mrs. Goodbody said. No more speaking now unless spoken to . . ."

Dressed starkly in a black suit with a white shirt and thin black tie, John Ramsay looked as if he were going through some great emotional crisis and was in imminent danger of collapse. He appeared to be gliding along in some kind of catatonic trance and was piloted through the shadows to the table by his guardian and protector, Mrs. Goodbody, and seated there.

Mrs. Goodbody took her seat, gazed imperiously round the table, then nodded her head; everyone obediently placed their hands flat on the table.

Under lowered eyelids, David glanced furtively at the people seated closest to him and wondered if anyone else shared his discomfiture. Much and all as he admired and respected Edwina Charles, this, he decided, was definitely not his scene. He felt ridiculous.

He took another quick look, this time right round the table; when his eyes finally lighted on Ramsay, he felt himself cringe inwardly. The man looked as though he were having a seizure: he was actually foaming at the mouth.

Transfixed, David continued to watch him. The medium's glazed, staring eyes grew larger: then, with a terrible rasping gasp, he slumped forward, his forehead striking the tabletop with a sickening thud.

David winced and looked quickly at Mrs. Charles, whose own eyes were fixed imperturbably on the medium.

My God! marvelled David as he watched her. *Now I know for sure I'll never understand her!*

Ramsay had started moaning and was now bumping his forehead repeatedly on the table. And with sufficient force, David noted, to dislodge the hairpiece he was wearing.

Fascinated, David watched the hairpiece inch its way across Ramsay's scalp until it was hanging down over one ear and prayed that he would be able to stop himself from laughing out loud if it fell off altogether.

Ramsay's moaning increased, and the table became increasingly bespeckled with foam from his mouth as his head crashed down on it time and again.

No wonder Mrs. Goodbody was concerned for the man, thought David, himself becoming anxious for him. Much more of this and Ramsay would knock himself senseless!

With a strangulated cry, which sent icy chills tingling down David's spine, Ramsay fell still across the table. Then, after what seemed an interminable length of time, he made a series of clipped, inarticulate sounds, which Mrs. Goodbody promptly interpreted, in an abrupt undertone, as belonging to the now dead language of an extinct tribe of Aztec Indians. And which, she then went on to explain, was being spoken here tonight (through John Ramsay) by Ulla, the medium's spirit control.

David gave Mrs. Charles a startled, questioning glance, which she ignored, leaving him to ponder alone over the problem of how they were going to be able to interpret an obscure dead language to get their answers.

There was a brief pause, then Mrs. Goodbody looked at Mrs. Charles and said, "The medium is ready to begin now. You may speak to him. But please remember to moderate your voice."

Mrs. Charles nodded that she understood. "I wish," she said softly but clearly, "to make contact with the spirit of Rendell Maxwell Pym. Is this possible tonight, please?"

A silence was followed by a long string of muted, indistinguishable utterances from the medium, rather more than David for one would have thought were necessary to convey the simple yes which Mrs. Goodbody translated from them.

"Is Rendell Pym there?" asked Mrs. Charles.

Mrs. Goodbody frowned quickly as the medium muttered something. "I think—" she paused, inclined her head on one side, and listened intently to Ramsay's garbled mutterings. "No, the man you wish to speak to tonight is not there, Ulla says."

"Does Ulla know why the spirit of Rendell Pym is not

willing to make itself known to us tonight?" inquired Mrs. Charles.

Mrs. Goodbody and the others waited expectantly, but there was no response from the medium to this question.

Mrs. Charles tried again. "Could Ulla perhaps try to reach Rendell Pym for me and tell him that some old friends and acquaintances of his have come here specially tonight to speak with him?"

Again they all looked expectantly at Ramsay and waited, and this time he responded.

Mrs. Goodbody leaned forward a little and listened attentively to what he had to say. "We seem to be getting some interference," she said after a moment. "I am not sure, but I am getting a name—Purdah, I think. . . . No—" She leaned suddenly forward again as the medium muttered something else. *"Purdie.* Does that name mean anything to any of you?" she asked with a frown.

Dolly Dackers spoke up. "Roger Purdie?" She looked quickly at Mrs. Charles, who nodded to her to go ahead. "Roger?" said Dolly. "It's Dolly here, Dolly Dackers. Remember me?"

There was a long silence, and then the medium abruptly gave a muffled grunt.

Mrs. Goodbody indicated to Dolly Dackers that she could continue.

"Do you have a message for us, Roger?" asked Dolly.

Mrs. Goodbody frowned anxiously over the medium's agitated and protracted response.

"There seems to be something wrong," she said. "I can't quite make out what it is." She paused, looked at the medium apprehensively. "Something about a dog, I think. Does that mean anything to anyone?"

Fullbright said (a little too loudly and was cautioned with a heavy frown of disapproval from nearly everyone), "That could be Blackie, my dog."

"Is Blackie with Mr. Purdie?" asked Mrs. Charles, watching the medium closely.

There was no response from Ramsay.

Mrs. Charles waited, but the silence only lengthened. Mrs. Goodbody looked at her expectantly and then invited her with her eyes to continue.

"Could Ulla ask Mr. Purdie who killed Mr. Fullbright's dog?" inquired Mrs. Charles.

Mrs. Goodbody shook her head anxiously over the medium's reaction to this question. He was greatly agitated. The muscles under the eye on the side of his face exposed to view went into a severe spasm, which gave the impression that, although Ramsay's head was perfectly motionless on the table, he was nevertheless under attack from something and flinching away from it.

Ramsay's lips worked slackly, a few garbled utterances escaped.

"Ulla warns that you must speak no more of dogs tonight," said Mrs. Goodbody quickly. "There are terrible cross vibrations . . . *pain.*" She frowned. "Would anybody know of any injury . . . yes," she said, leaning forward quickly with a faint moan of her own. "A wound inflicted by some vicious beast . . . near the right eye, I think."

"Purdie," whispered Dolly Dackers. "He had a scar under his right eye from a dog bite he got when he was a child."

"The spirits are becoming greatly distressed," announced Mrs. Goodbody in a very matter-of-fact voice. "I very much regret that I am going to have to terminate this rather abruptly. Mr. Ramsay is in terrible torment. I cannot let things go too far. I dare not for his sake."

Mrs. Charles, to whom these remarks were addressed, nodded and said quickly, "There was just the one question, if that would be possible?"

Mrs. Goodbody frowned concernedly at the prostrate form lying across the table; then, apparently having heard something which the medium had said and which had escaped everyone else's ears, she replied abruptly, "Yes," and then added her earlier warning about terminating the seance.

"Is there some reason why the spirit of Rendell Pym cannot be here with us tonight, Ulla? If you cannot answer me, can you give us a sign?" asked the clairvoyante.

Ramsay was promptly taken by an uncontrollable fit of shuddering. The table quaked under his violently trembling body, and first one and then another of the people seated round it retracted their hands as if in mute protest at his lack of self-restraint.

"The seance is over for tonight," said Mrs. Goodbody peremptorily. She rose and bent over the now perfectly still and quiet medium. "Mr. Ramsay is absolutely exhausted. I fear we may have overtaxed his strength. Please do not move from your seats for a few moments."

She assisted Ramsay to straighten his spine and then, with a sigh, he collapsed back in his chair.

Mrs. Goodbody hovered over him, searching his face anxiously. His head had sagged onto his chest, and he was wheezing asthmatically. Gradually, however, his breathing became less stertorous, and he appeared to be sleeping.

A deathly silence fell over the entire company. Everyone's attention was focused on the medium, who had raised his head and was slowly coming round. He looked less tired, an entirely different person almost from the one who had emerged from the anteroom only a short while earlier. Colour was returning to his cheeks, his eyelids were fluttering, and once his eyes had remained wide open in a fixed stare for thirty seconds before drooping closed again.

A remarkable performance, thought David, who was feeling slightly nauseated by the whole affair. He would be glad when it was all over. Sometimes—

David felt the hairs growing on the back of his neck stand on end. His eyes were drawn hypnotically across the hall to the entrance doorway.

Two glassy eyes stared back at him out of the gloom. A soft rumbling sound suddenly became a low, menacing snarl, and Fullbright spoke for nearly everyone when he muttered, *"What the devil was that?"* He twisted round in his chair and looked in the direction of the sound, which was coming from behind him.

Out of the shadows stepped a uniformed police officer—a dog handler—and a large Alsatian. They started to cross the hall.

"I'm sorry if we startled you," the police officer apologised, still walking towards the platform. "We were just passing, and I noticed that the front door wasn't locked. I couldn't see any lights, and I wondered if the premises had been broken into."

"It's all right, Officer," said David, and almost as one person, everyone let out a deep sigh of relief.

As it neared the platform, the dog at the police officer's side bared its teeth and the hackles rose on its neck.

"I hope you've got that dog under control, Officer," remarked the clairvoyante. "He seems terribly agitated about something."

As she spoke, Mrs. Charles casually turned her head and fixed her gaze on Dolly Dackers, the only one besides herself who was not staring at the police officer and his dog. Dolly Dackers was looking searchingly at the man sitting directly opposite her. A whole range of expressions crossed her face —puzzlement, bewilderment, realisation, incredulity— slowly to begin with, and then, when she finally acknowledged the evidence of her eyes and accepted it as being the truth, she thrust herself back from the table with her hands. Her chair scraped noisily along the wooden floor, and everyone looked questioningly at her as she stumbled wildly to her feet.

The dog handler and the Alsatian paused before the platform, Fullbright's head swinging round in a reflex action as the menacing growls in the animal's throat reached a crescendo of malevolent antagonism.

"Pym," gasped Dolly Dackers. She backed away from the table, her hands pushed out in front of her as if to ward off something horribly evil and malignant. *"You're Rendell Pym!"*

CHAPTER TWENTY-THREE

Martin Fullbright's head shot round to the front. His eyes met Dolly Dackers's and held them steadfastly.

The dog's velvety black muzzle rucked up into a ferocious snarl, and its strong white teeth flashed a warning.

In another reflex action, Fullbright grabbed the edge of the table in both hands and scrambled to his feet, knocking over his chair.

Startled by Fullbright's sudden movement and the unexpected clatter of the falling chair, the dog reared up at him. Fullbright's arms flew up protectively, and then the obscenities poured forth, in the voice of the man known as Martin Fullbright, but from out of the twisted mind of Rendell Pym.

"Bristowe," said the police officer quietly, and the dog came obediently to heel.

"Well, Mr. Pym?" said the clairvoyante evenly when finally, his rage spent, Rendell Pym fell silent.

He dropped his arms and stared at her. Then he grinned his awful grin and let his gaze sweep malevolently round the table and over Dolly Dackers. *"Prove it!"* he snarled.

"Oh, I don't need to prove it, Mr. Pym," said the clairvoyante. "You saved everyone that bother when you killed Rosa Trumble's dog. I can imagine what pleasure that must have given you after having had to suffer his company these past two years. And you did have to suffer him, didn't you, Mr. Pym? Because one day that dog was going to be your alibi. How could Martin Fullbright possibly be suspected of murdering the other principal players in the Pym murder trial drama—the other two wise monkeys (the doctor and the judge)—when he was lying apparently unconscious all night beside the body of his faithful old dog after having himself been attacked by the dog's and their killer? This was supposing, of course, that someday someone—another Tony Manners, perhaps—would see the connection between Dr. MacDonald's and Mr. Justice Halahan's deaths."

Mrs. Charles paused, then smiled faintly. "But you weren't lying there on the common with your dog, were you, Mr. Pym? Early the following morning, yes, when an elderly, well-known marathon runner stumbled across you and the dog—a man who exercises along a set route through the quiet streets and common land of Lymstead every morning at that hour—but not at eleven o'clock the previous night, when you should have been there with the dead dog. There is a witness, Mr. Pym—the young man who, as the police say, has been helping them with their inquiries into the murder of Roger Purdie and also, as one would expect once the police realised that the same person had committed the two crimes, the attack on you a short while before on the common.

"Only there wasn't any attack on you, was there? The injury to your head you inflicted upon yourself. . . . Perhaps only a small wound to begin with, just a big enough gash to give you a little of your blood, a few hairs from your head, some particles of skin—the kind of evidence you knew the police would expect to find on the weapon which you had used to bludgeon your dog to death and claimed had also been used on you.

"As you are only too well aware, the police already know that this witness, Trevor Flegg—the innocent young man whom you would happily send to prison for your crimes—was on the common around eleven o'clock that night. No doubt foolishly—though one could perhaps understand his motivation, the hostility he felt towards the police whom he did not trust to believe him or to treat him fairly when the evidence against him was so overwhelming—he did not tell them what he saw as he crossed the common. Or rather, what he did *not* see.

"It was you he didn't see, Mr. Pym. He saw your dead dog, but you weren't there. And you couldn't have been, could you? You couldn't have been there, lying unconscious on the common, and at The Ugly Duckling—in two places at once —could you?"

Pym sneered at her. "Got a right bee in your bonnet about Pym, haven't you? I could tell that the day you and Sayer came to see me. You're not even a gifted amateur—I take back what I said about you the other day—if you really think anybody's going to believe that that young lout Flegg didn't kill Purdie. Purdie was Pym's friend, his only friend. Purdie even perjured himself to save Pym's skin—"

"But not at the trial," said Mrs. Charles. "The coercion that came to light later on had, I believe, been put on Purdie to tell the truth at the trial, not to lie, so that Fullbright would be assured of his conviction. It was when the tide began to turn in Pym's favour and Mrs. Dackers felt safe to come forward and tell the truth about Mr. Krendel and his relationship with Mrs. Pym, and handed over the diary which had been removed from the scene of the crime by Mr. Krendel, that Purdie climbed aboard the bandwagon, as it were, and turned the tables on Fullbright by telling the lie that but for Fullbright he would have willingly told at the trial.

"Yes, Mr. Pym, Roger Purdie was a true friend. But not to the end, I fear. That was why you killed him, wasn't it? He went out to The Grange to warn Martin Fullbright that he suspected that Rendell Pym was alive. And the reason why he suspected that you were still alive was that he, like Tony Manners, had made the connection between the deaths of Dr. MacDonald and Mr. Justice Halahan and the threat Pym had made to avenge himself on his three wise monkeys.

"Ellen Purdie has told me of her father's visit to The Grange several days before he was murdered and that he was greatly upset afterwards. I don't think he recognised you, Mr. Pym. He, like everyone else, probably never for one moment doubted that he was speaking to Martin Fullbright."

Mrs. Charles paused, her eyebrows rose. "So what made him suddenly change sides? Was it because of Tony Manners —because he guessed that Rendell Pym had also killed her?"

Mrs. Charles eyed Pym speculatively, then slowly nodded her head. "He drew the line at that, didn't he? She'd been on your side, hadn't she? Undoubtedly would've spoken up for you at your trial if Fullbright had let her. And that, I think, troubled Roger Purdie's conscience. There's no doubt in my mind that he didn't like Fullbright—no one did. But what better way to make up for the girl's death—which wasn't playing fair in Purdie's book—than by giving Fullbright a sporting chance to save himself?"

Mrs. Charles smiled coldly. "You must have really hated him for that, Mr. Pym. Though I daresay that by now you were beginning to become a little alarmed, weren't you? First Tony Manners, and now Purdie. Despite all the care and skill you had displayed in committing your crimes, people were beginning to suspect. And, of course, the moment someone began to entertain these suspicions, the greater the risk of your true identity being revealed. And Roger Purdie would've undoubtedly been a bigger risk than most, especially since he had proved himself to be a turncoat. He therefore had to be eliminated, and the simplest way of achieving this was to mask the real motive for his murder by killing him in conjunction with the alleged attack on yourself."

"You're grasping at straws," said Pym with a derisive laugh.

"No, Mr. Pym. No more than Tony Manners was when she read about the death of Mr. Justice Halahan and recalled what Dr. MacDonald's former housekeeper had told her of the doctor's murder. Tony went straight out to see Mr. Bing. She did not know the connection between Mr. Bing and Mr. Justice Halahan—that Mr. Bing had been the judge's clerk, that is—until Mr. Bing told her, but she guessed that the message the judge had given Mr. Ramsay for Mr. Bing referred to you, Mr. Pym, and not to the pain he had been suffering.

"Greatly alarmed by Tony's allegations of not one murder, but two—Dr. MacDonald's as well—Mr. Bing waited until Tony had gone, and then he got in touch with you—or rather, ex-Detective Chief Superintendent Martin Fullbright, Rosa Trumble's brother—and told you about Tony's visit and the wild claims that she had been making, her suspicion that Rendell Pym was still alive.

"You allayed Mr. Bing's fears—assured him, as you assured Mr. Sayer and myself, that Pym was dead and that nobody could put anything like a faked death over an old police dog like you—and then, realising how grave your situation was and that Tony Manners, as a former W.P.C., might at any moment take her suspicions to the police, you went straight out and killed her. You followed her, boarded the same express train to Scotland, and then pushed her off it before she could take her investigations into Dr. MacDonald's death any further.

"I even think it's possible that you gave evidence at her inquest disguised as a Scot—the last person who saw her alive. You had got away with it once before, when you had played the part of the American tourist who raised the alarm about Dr. MacDonald after finding his body in a Glasgow graveyard, and again, I believe, with Mr. Justice Halahan, when you lunched with him and discussed the Pym trial. 'Mr. Janus,' a New Zealand author, you were calling yourself this time. And not by chance, I would venture to say—Janus being the Roman god who had two faces, one at the front and one at the back.

"I think you really went there that day to familiarise yourself with the judge's home before you returned that night to kill him—the night you, alias Mr. Janus, alias Martin Fullbright (Rosa Trumble's brother), knew that the butler would

be attending a spiritualists' meeting in Lymstead and that
the judge would be more or less alone in the house.

"And then, just to make everything neat and tidy—in case
one day someone looked back and saw the possibility that
Rendell Pym might have come back from the dead, so to
speak, and murdered his three wise monkeys—you made
sure that when Martin Fullbright and his dog were discovered on the common, it would be by an elderly man. This
time a genuine elderly man, an athlete whose training route
and whose hours you were familiar with. The fact that he
was genuine served the main purpose of giving instant cred-
ibility to all the other elderly men who had been at or
around the scene of Rendell Pym's other crimes."

"You're mad," said Pym.

David, who, along with everyone else, had been watching
and listening to proceedings in a state of numbed shock,
suddenly recovered himself and said, "The game's up, Pym.
You might as well accept it."

"I'm afraid so, Mr. Pym," said Mrs. Charles quietly. "You
know as well as I do that the police will now get in touch
with Rose Trumble—bring her back to England, if necessary. And she won't be so easily fooled as the rest of us were.
She knew both men intimately. Rendell Pym *and* Martin
Fullbright."

The clairvoyante paused and studied Pym thoughtfully.
"It was a brilliant disguise, Mr. Pym. Though one made
considerably easier for you to adopt successfully because
basically you and Martin Fullbright were so alike in appearance, with the same heavy bone structure, the same broad,
wide forehead and large hands"—Mrs. Charles refrained
from making any comparison between the two men and
Neanderthal man, but it was ever present in her mind as she
looked at Rendell Pym—"a full head of hair. . . . Yours, of
course, went grey very early during your breakdown—
which, incidentally, I do believe you suffered though nowhere near as seriously as you pretended."

She hesitated, then eyed his thick head of hair speculatively. "Perhaps you were even telling Mr. Sayer and me the truth when you said Rendell Pym's hair fell out through ill health, but if it did, then in time it all grew back again."

Ramsay suddenly spoke. While no one had been watching, his hairpiece had surreptitiously found its way neatly back into place on top of his scalp.

"But Mr. Fullbright—I mean, that man standing there," he added, nodding his head at Rendell Pym, "came to see us soon after Mrs. Trumble emigrated to Australia." Ramsay looked to Mrs. Goodbody for support, and she gave it to him in the form of a vigorous nod of her head and an emphatic, "Yes, that's the man."

The clairvoyante said, "No, Mr. Ramsay. That man was and is Rendell Pym. Martin Fullbright was dead, murdered by Rendell Pym the day Martin Fullbright's sister Rosa left for Australia. Martin Fullbright, the senior police officer in charge of the Pamela Pym murder investigation, was both one of Rendell Pym's victims and the man into whose life he would step and use as his cover for the other murders he planned to commit later on. It was Martin Fullbright who fell to his death under a train."

Mrs. Charles turned her gaze full on Pym.

"Shall I tell you what I believe happened that day, Mr. Pym? You tricked Fullbright into leaving the nursing home with you. Fullbright was, by this time, completely hood-winked by your cunningly contrived metamorphosis—not in your physical appearance, as you would have had Mr. Sayer and me believe when we visited you at the hospital last week, but in your personality, Pym's apparent desire to be left in peace to tend the garden at the nursing home and to be allowed to organise the home's social functions.

"For all his faults, Fullbright was, in the main, I think, a shrewdly observant policeman, but he was unable to see himself as you and so many other people saw him. Fullbright never realised how physically alike you and he were and how easy it would be for you, 'a gifted actor,' I remember you said"—she smiled thinly—"to impersonate him. The

fact that Fullbright was by now only partially sighted posed
no problem for you at all. Just what does 'partially sighted'
mean, anyway? Very little to the ordinary fully sighted person like myself, who simply assumes that someone so afflicted can see but not so well as I am able to, whereas
complete blindness would have made things much more
difficult, if not indeed quite impossible, for you.

"However, after somehow succeeding in tricking Fullbright into accompanying you that day, you no doubt
knocked him unconscious, perhaps even killed him,
changed clothes with him, and then heaved him over the
parapet of the railway footbridge into the path of an oncoming train. You then returned to the nursing home, not as
Rendell Pym, but as Martin Fullbright, and raised the alarm
about Pym, whom you claimed had gone missing.

"You, and no doubt several of the remaining patients at
the nursing home, as you claimed, went out on your search
for Pym. You found what purported to be his body on the
railway line. Martin Fullbright was a good few years older
than you, but the trauma of your trial—a trial which I believe you thought you should never have had to face because
in your own twisted mind you believed the murder of your
faithless young wife was justified—and your subsequent
breakdown had somewhat hastened certain of the ageing
processes so that you easily passed for a man considerably
older than you really were.

"And then, after you had made the formal identification of
the remains on the railway line—which identification was
accepted without question (who was going to question the
word of someone as responsible as Martin Fullbright, an ex-
detective chief superintendent of police and a man who had
both lived with and known Rendell Pym intimately for approximately eight years?)—you returned to the nursing
home and thereafter continued to live your life as your arch-
protagonist, the police officer who had carried out the investigation into the murder of your wife, remaining on at the

nursing home as its caretaker when the property changed hands and became a day school."

Mrs. Charles paused and gave Pym a wintry smile. "It was a brilliantly conceived plan, and, but for the young woman whom Fullbright I've no doubt genuinely considered too soft for police work, you almost got away with it."

Rendell Pym seemed to measure everyone up with his eye, as if calculating his chances of making a run for it, but before he could follow through with any action, the police dog, acting intuitively, began straining on its leash and snapping at his ankles.

Rendell Pym's shoulders sagged momentarily, and briefly he looked a very old, tired man. He stared at the dog, the dog stared back at him; then, squaring his shoulders and straightening his tie, Rendell Pym turned to the police officer and said, "My name is Martin Edmund Fullbright. I am seventy-one years of age. I live in the caretaker's flat at the Brayside Infants School. I was formerly a detective chief superintendent of police stationed at Lymstead, and latterly at Uppingham . . ."

He went on, slowly and clearly, giving his, Martin Fullbright's, personal details.

Neville Krendel, pushing back his chair, got to his feet and said, "He's off. It's going to be the old trial all over again. Only this time he'll be acting the part of a policeman. I can't sit through any more of this, I'm going to get my pipe," he finished, with a sour look at Mrs. Goodbody which defied her to try and stop him.

CHAPTER TWENTY-FOUR

"You knew all along that Roger Purdie wasn't Pym," said David Sayer.

Mrs. Charles rose from the flower bed which she had been weeding and took off her gardening gloves, balanced them on the handle of the fork stuck in the earth nearby. Smiling faintly, she said, "Purdie's initials were the same, and you know what they say about people who assume a new name and identity. As often as not they'll keep their own initials. And from the description Ellen Purdie gave me of her father, he was very like Pym physically. And he didn't like dogs. But then again, neither does Neville Krendel. Though I must say that in his case that dreadful beard of his would've been a wee bit heavy-handed if it were really part of an overall disguise. Pym was far too subtle an actor to resort to that sort of thing. Yet I think Krendel would have been a natural choice for Pym to eliminate and then impersonate had it not been for Krendel's continuing association with Dolly Dackers. Though oddly enough," she shrugged, "Pym didn't appear to bear any real grudge against the other men in his wife's life. He only felt aggrieved with the people who challenged his right to sort out his domestic problems in his own way. He'd never have got such a heavy sentence if Fullbright hadn't suppressed the truth about Mrs. Pym's affairs. And perhaps in time," she sighed, "he would've even picked up the threads of his acting career. But unfortunately, the police investigation and the trial, the way they were conducted, and being fired from his television role so summarily turned his brain."

"If you ask me he was always a bit touched."

"Probably. Genius and madness are often one and the same thing. And he was a genius . . . as an actor, I mean."

David nodded. "Yes, I've got to hand it to him there. It was a brilliant impersonation, like you said."

"Yes. And do you know why it was so brilliant?" she asked. "Because with only one or two exceptions, he was always telling us the truth. That was the real secret of the success of Pym's impersonation of Martin Fullbright. All Pym had to do was to tell the truth about himself—which he knew better than anybody else. When he said Pym was guilty of the murder for which he had been tried, he knew it was the truth because he had committed the murder. He was really talking to us not as Fullbright the policeman, but as Pym the murderer."

"Seems a terrible waste of the taxpayers' money taking him to court again. Krendel had it pretty well summed up, I thought. It'll be the same old fiasco all over again. And that devil Pym is so crafty that even if they shut him away in a maximum security prison with a dozen psychiatrists dancing attendance on him, he'll talk his way out again. I can even see him enjoying the challenge. Be child's play after what he did with his three wise monkeys."

David shook his head. "Talk about a brassneck . . . The way he left sticking plaster over the eyes, ear, and mouth of each of his victims and then planted himself—with the one notable exception that you spotted—at the scene of his crimes. Which, as Merton pointed out, could be said to imply a certain contempt for the police and their powers of deduction. Rather a perceptive comment, I thought. . . . In the circumstances," he grinned.

"I must call in some time and thank him for his assistance with the police officer and the dog."

"I wouldn't do that just yet, Madame," said David with a grave smile.

"No, perhaps not," she said, smiling back at him. "He's let Trevor Flegg go?"

"With a warning. Gave him a right flea in his ear, by all

accounts, for not telling him that Fullbright was nowhere near his dead dog. Merton was so mad about it he would've had a charge brought against him for obstructing the true course of justice if it hadn't been for you and his fear of what you might do to him if he went for the lad. You'll never get Merton to say thank you, but in his own funny little way, he's grateful to you and the Lymstead Spiritualists—and to your mysterious sentimental Mr. Valentine—for keeping mum about the mess he made, or would've made of everything, if it hadn't been for your intervention."

"The spiritualists' (and my) motives—not to mention Jimmy Valentine's," she smiled, "mightn't have been quite so pure as you could be thinking. There is some publicity that we can all well do without."

"Did you ever get to the bottom of the mystery over Valentine and find out what his real connection with the girl was?"

She nodded. "It was more or less as you suspected. He gave Mr. Manners the information about the big jewel robbery you mentioned and then squared his debt to him for never having revealed the source of his information by always keeping a protective eye on his daughter. Valentine claimed he would have finished up at the bottom of a river wearing concrete shoes, I believe he said, if it hadn't been for Mr. Manners's keeping quiet about him."

David shook his head. "You have an interesting circle of friends, Madame." He looked at the time. "And talking about spiritualists . . . Rosa Trumble was due to arrive at Heathrow early this morning. They should've fetched her up here by now. Rather a distressing business for her, I shouldn't wonder. They're going to dig up her brother's body, you know."

"I think she'll cope," said Mrs. Charles.

"Yes." He was quiet for a moment. "That was something I noticed at the seance the other night. A sort of resignation . . . Or was it a sense of inevitability?"

"No, Superintendent. Acceptance. The true spiritualist

goes with the flow and accepts without question that which another cannot."

"It's all too deep and devious for me," he confessed. "Now if you'd told me you'd used some form of blackmail to get everybody to turn up there that night, I could believe that." He waited, eyed her expectantly, but she merely smiled without answering.

"You're not going to tell me you didn't rig that seance the other night? All that head banging and that business about Purdie's dog bite giving Ramsay a pain in the eye . . ." He wagged his head at her. *"Never!* That's all a bit like the Dixons and their mothballs. You've got as much chance of convincing me that that seance was genuine as your brother has of getting me to believe that the way to get rid of moles is with mothballs!"

Mrs. Charles smiled to herself. "It worked for him, Superintendent. Moles don't drop out of the skies—"

"I know, they just keep moving right on down the road," he said grimly, and they both laughed.

ABOUT THE AUTHOR

MIGNON WARNER was born in Australia but now lives in England with her husband, whom she assists in the invention, design, and manufacture of magic apparatus. She spends most of her free time pursuing her interest in psychic research and the occult. Her previous novels about the clairvoyante Mrs. Charles include *Illusion*, *Devil's Knell*, and *The Girl Who Was Clairvoyant*.